From the Ashes

From the Ashes

PAT RAMSEY BECKMAN

ROBERTS RINEHART PUBLISHERS
BOULDER, COLORADO
in cooperation with
THE COUNCIL FOR INDIAN EDUCATION

ISBN 1-57098-011-X

Library of Congress Catalog Number 95-69275

Published in the United States by
Roberts Rinehart Publishers
5455 Spine Road, Boulder, Colorado 80301

Published in Ireland by
Roberts Rinehart
Trinity House, Charleston Road
Dublin 6, Ireland

Distributed in the
U.S. and Canada by
Publishers Group West

Contents

+ + +

+ + +

✢ ✢ ✢

The Council for Indian Education Series

THE COUNCIL FOR INDIAN EDUCATION is a non-profit organization devoted to teacher training and to the publication of materials to aid in Indian education. All books are selected by an Indian editorial board and are approved for use with Indian children. Proceeds are used for the publication of more books for Indian children. Roberts Rinehart Publishers copublishes select manuscripts to aid the Council for Indian Education in the distribution of these books to wider markets, to aid in the production of books, and to support the Council's educational programs.

✢ ✢ ✢

Introduction

✦ ✦ ✦

The story is set in Ohio in 1794, the time of the Battle of Fallen Timbers between U.S. troops, led by General Anthony Wayne, and the Shawnee, led by Chief Blue Jacket.

The area at the fork of the Maumee and Auglaise Rivers in Defiance, Ohio is the location. This was the gathering place of the Indian tribes and their great war chiefs, Little Turtle, Blue Jacket, and Buckgonhelas.

Against this background, I have placed my story of David and Michael Godfrey Joyce. My inspiration for this story came from the discovery of two graves and a log cabin nestled between the Maumee and Little Tiffin River near my home in Defiance. In studying the abstracts of the land, I learned that the graves belonged to settlers who had lived in the cabin, and that their two sons were adopted by Potawatomie Indians in the early 1800s. Although the name Godfrey appears in the abstracts, this is not the story of the Godfrey family. The name was chosen by coincidence, perhaps a trick of memory.

Historians debate the origins of Chief Blue Jacket. The belief that he was a white man captured by the

Shawnees and that he later became known as Chief Blue Jacket has enjoyed wide acceptance since 1967. Some historians now believe he was a full-blooded Shawnee.

The stump of the old apple tree beside Sun-Will-Shine's (Cooh-cooh-Cheeh, the Medicine Woman) bark hut still remains by the Maumee River in Defiance, Ohio. During the summer of 1994 there was a bicentennial (200 years) celebration of the battle of Fallen Timbers and a commemoration of all the history surrounding this battle. A library now stands at the forks of the Maumee and Auglaize Rivers, still commanding the view, just as the troops and Shawnee Indians did 200 years ago.

I am deeply grateful to Randall L. Buchman, Professor of History at The Defiance College, Definace, Ohio, for setting me on the path of the story of Blue Jacket, and for approving my manuscript.

1

✛

Renegades

Davey was headed for the woodpile when he heard the noise. It sounded like footsteps dragging through dead, wet leaves. He'd lived here by the Tiffin River long enough to know it could be Shawnee renegades.

The Shawnees were mostly peaceful hunters who lived on the Maumee and Auglaize rivers. Davey's pa had come from the east to fur trade, and many times Davey had gone with him to George Ironside's trading post at the forks of the rivers and seen the Indian village.

But it was 1794 near the Great Lakes wilderness, and Davey knew war was coming for the peaceful Shawnee. The Indians and the white settlers were about to have a showdown over land, and the fur traders—including Davey's pa—were in trouble.

Quickly he climbed into the dark hollow of a sycamore tree and held his breath. At fifteen he, David Godfrey Joyce, was lean and too tall to fit easily into the hole. As he tried to stuff himself inside the tree, he scraped the bark. Did the renegades hear him? Quietly he drew one knee up to his chin and waited.

Pa had just told him to fetch firewood for supper, and eight-year-old Michael was helping Ma pour corn pudding into clay pots. Davey had to warn them. But how? The cricket sound he and his little brother used in the woods might work. Michael always played Indian games with Davey, tracking his footsteps, grinning that wide smile and pushing a tangle of straw-colored curls out of his eyes. But Davey couldn't get any sounds past the lump of fear in his throat. How else could he get Michael's attention?

Just then Davey noticed his bow leaning against the cabin. Cautiously he reached for it. But it was no use, he couldn't move without making a noise. Footsteps drew closer. Moon shadows darted between skeleton trees. Then he saw them — renegade Indians with long hair across their brown shoulders.

As he twisted around to get a clear view of the cabin, he sniffed smoke. Suddenly an Indian jumped from the cabin doorway dragging a sack. It was alive with muffled cries. When he realized Michael was in the sack, Davey started to jump from his hiding place. He wanted to shout, to leap in front of the renegade Indians and rip the sack from their hands. But he felt frozen, his mind screaming at him to move, his body stiff as the tree where he hid. Swiftly the renegades left on cat-like feet.

Now flames were shooting through the cabin door. They licked around the logs and darted through the windows. Davey's eyes burned from the smoke as he squeezed himself out of the hole. The tongues of fire grew, lapping around the dry pine wood, curling over the windowsills and up through the loft, devouring the little cabin.

"Ma! Pa!" he screamed, then grabbed a bucket and

cut through the trees to the little Tiffin River. He dipped the bucket into the shallow stream, sloshing water as he scaled the short hill to the house. "Ma! Pa!" he sobbed.

But scorching heat kept Davey back. Helpless, he fell to his knees. What was the matter with him? Sobs were catching in his throat now. Why didn't he just holler when he saw those Indians?

When the flames finally died down, he summoned all his strength and inched through the hot ashes on his knees. But it was too late. When he found them lying in the old kitchen, his ma and pa were already dead.

He kicked at the charred logs, shoving them apart. "Michael," he cried, "where are you?" Then he remembered the sack and slumped by the huge iron pot, still swinging from a hook over the broken hearth.

Finally, Davey lifted his mother's frail body and carried her to the edge of the stream. His eyes and lungs burned from the smoke as he squinted at the moonlight glistening on the clear water that trailed by the cabin. It seemed so peaceful, as if nothing had happened.

Suddenly a cold shiver shook him. He was afraid. He went back for his pa and laid him gently next to his ma on the cold ground. Only a few hours ago, they had been happily preparing the evening meal. *Where can I go?* he wondered. *Where's Michael?* He curled up next to his ma and pa and closed his eyes.

A powder coat of April snow tipped the tender grass with white-morning sparkle when he woke. His eyes were open, but the nightmare was still there. He stood up and watched the last thin plume of smoke trail toward the sky. Then he realized what he had to do. With a giant ache in his heart he buried his parents, too sickened to even breathe a prayer.

A chill rippled his body as he plunged his clammy hands into his pockets where he felt something soft— buzzard down his ma had given him in case he got hurt in the woods. What good would buzzard down do now? It wouldn't stop the emptiness, the sickening ache in his gut.

It had always been hard living here, not like the civilized home in the east when he was little, where his ma had taught school and his pa had been a printer. Tears welled in Davey's eyes as he remembered his ma's softness. *Michael's going to need me,* he thought. *I've got to find my brother.*

He looked toward the charred cabin. Ma had tried to prepare him to go on without her and pa. "The Lord said, remember, I am with you always," she told him. "Seek and you shall find. Ask and you shall receive. Knock and it shall be opened unto you." He could hear the music in her voice reciting those scriptures, telling them about the Lord taking care of them. But she probably never thought he and Michael would be separated. Where *was* Michael?

Davey struggled to organize his thoughts. He would find Ironside, he decided, stretching the aches from his legs. *He'll help me find my brother.* He stuffed his shirttail in his pants. His raccoon hat was still on the ground by the tree where he'd hidden from the renegades. How ashamed he felt. The shame gnawed at him with pain he had never known. His pa had always told him how strong and brave he was. How he was really going to be somebody someday. And he had come to believe it.

His mother often said that if he hadn't been born so handsome, he'd fit right in with those tobacco-chewin' traders. The more ripped his linsey pants and the more uncombed his hair, the stronger he felt. Sometimes he tied a yellow band around his black hair and stuck a chicken feather in it. It made him feel like the Indians he admired.

He blinked hard and shoved his hat over his black hair. "They can't be dead!" His throat felt swollen fighting back the tears, and he couldn't swallow.

The arrows Davey and Michael had been making out of bone and turkey feathers still lay on top of the wood pile, but his bow had gone to ashes. He turned away.

The little Tiffin flowed by smooth and clear. Davey looked back at the place once more, wiping his sleeve across his eyes, then waded into water just over his knees to avoid the low branches along the bank. For a while he followed the shallow creek. He knew it led into the wide Maumee River that flowed past Ironside's trading post on the east bank, and the peace woman's hut on the north bank, and forked with the Auglaize. Directly opposite Ironside's post on the Auglaize was the Shawnee village — wegiwas of Chief Blue Jacket's tribe, and fields for planting corn.

He remembered seeing Sun-Will-Shine's hut nested on the bank like a giant mushroom under a spreading apple tree, and behind it a small corn garden tended by Shawnee women and children. Beyond the peace woman's hut, at the top of a hill stood the long Council House where Chiefs of many tribes held important meetings.

Davey recalled seeing the happy natives when he visited the trader, Ironside, with his pa. But he also knew there was trouble brewing between them and the new settlers, and that there were turncoats and renegades on both sides.

Pa had said there was talk of another battle for land, and the settlers and Indians were both nervous. Better be careful, Davey thought, as he trotted along the bank swinging his arms in rhythm to his pounding feet.

As he rounded a bend, something moved in the trees. Then it was behind him. Davey swung around. His racoon hat fell to the ground. Pain, razor sharp, seared up the back of his head. Everything went black.

When he opened his eyes, Davey's head throbbed to his heartbeat. He was wedged between two figures in a canoe that wavered like reflections in the water.

Hands bound behind him, his head shoved down over his knees, he could just make out yellow war paint on the face to the rear. The Indians pulled paddles through the dark water as if stirring thick pudding.

One seems younger, Davey thought. *He's kind of short and dark. He's fiercer lookin', like a Mohawk. The other one's taller, about my age, a Shawnee maybe. Wonder if they have Michael too? No, they're too young to be those renegades.* Davey felt the knot on his head tighten. It was too hard to think anymore.

The dark Mohawk scowled. "*Maw scoute-cagah, maw teikou neapouthou.*"

Both scouts hopped out and yanked the canoe onto the mud. The taller one left, but returned with enough branches to make a fire. They stretched deerskins out around the fire. "*Skelouatheatha kikenecaw,*" said the Mohawk, hunching over the flames.

Davey knew some of the words from his ma who was good at languages. *Squawlawey* meant "I am hungry" and *Skelouatheatha kikenecaw* was "the boy is our prisoner."

Davey's stomach felt sick, and the hairs on the back of his neck stiffened. Frantically he twisted his wrists while

he watched them eat. It was dusk already, and he didn't
know where Michael was.

The Indian boys were shouting now. The Mohawk
drew his skinning knife across a black furry hide, held it
between his legs, chewed a strip of sinew till it got soft,
then threaded it through the fur.

He slapped it on his head, dancing and bending in a
circle. "*He-hie, he hie.*" The fire played in weird shapes
under his closed eyes. Red paint spots on his eyelids
made them look open.

Suddenly he was behind Davey, clutching his neck
and pressing cold steel against his throat.

Davey's mouth felt dry as chalk. "You going to kill
me?"

The short muscular Indian jerked him from the
canoe and dragged him to a tree. He threw a rope
around him, circling it around the tree till it coiled tight
like a snake to his neck, then rattled a pouch of deer
hooves next to his ear.

Davey struggled to get loose.

The taller brave tramped back and forth to a hickory,
pulling furs from a deep hole, piling them across his
arms, and slip-sliding down the bank to load the canoe.

Suddenly the Shawnee tripped and sprawled on his
face at Davey's feet. Blood spurted from his leg. Bits of
grass stuck to the scratches.

"*Squee,*" jeered the Mohawk, seemingly pleased at the
blood oozing.

"I can help you," said Davey.

The Shawnee eyed him suspiciously, then, seeing the
blood wouldn't stop, reached for Davey's ropes and
sliced them with his skinning blade.

Quickly Davey showed him the wad of buzzard down

from his pocket. "*Weynusee,* buzzard," he said, leaning over the scout's leg.

Davey made a tourniquet with his rope and tightened it at the Shawnee's crotch. "I'll wash it with water from the river. *Nepaalo,* lie down." He froze with fear watching his own white hand move across the Indian's dark skin. An ugly pointed stick stuck in the brave's leg. Davey forced himself to pull it out. He soaked the hole with water, and stuffed it with the soft feathers from his pocket, thanking his ma in the prayer he couldn't say at her grave.

The lean, handsome Indian didn't flinch. "I White Wolf," he said. "That half-brother, Black Wolf." He pointed to his stocky companion. "Peace Woman our mother. His father Mohawk, my father Shawnee." The injured Shawnee spoke slowly, gently.

Black Wolf shrugged. "Your white boy is like a woman, a coward like you."

Davey flinched at the word *coward,* but he was so relieved to hear White Wolf speak English that he picked up the friendly Indian's furs and slung them across his shoulder. No need to fear Black Wolf, he thought. He was a bully, and bullies are just show. He slipped his other arm around the scout's waist and they hobbled together down the bank. Finally settled in the canoe — Davey in the middle, White Wolf at the bow — Black Wolf pushed off toward the forks.

Soon Davey could see camp fires dancing against the twilight sky. Their reflections in the river reminded Davey of evenings spent fishing with his pa in the Tiffin, bonfires crackling on the edge and sparkling on the tips of ripples in the stream. In his mind, the big form of his pa hovered over him. He could almost smell his sweet tobacco.

As the canoe entered the deep waters of the Maumee River, Davey couldn't make out George Ironside's cabin. Something was wrong. The traders' camp was too quiet.

2

✝

Blue Jacket

As they pushed onto the Auglaize River bank, Black Wolf jumped from the boat. He bounded up the steep hill to the trader's cabin, leaving the furs for Davey and White Wolf to carry.

Davey knew Ironside paid the Indians for their furs with wampum — shell beads and jewelry. "Why don't you stay here and rest, White Wolf? I'll carry the furs up the bank for you."

"Good," answered the gentle White Wolf.

Black Wolf was already on his way back, spearing the ground with a gold-headed cane. "Pretty," he crooned, flashing a bright blue tortoise-shell box with inlaid pearls.

Davey saw only one miserable fur trader as he dumped the furs inside the cabin door. He was full of whiskey, feet propped and crossed on the splintery table. Ironside was nowhere in sight. "You seen Mr. Ironside?" he asked.

The whiskery old man burped and slumped to the side of his chair.

Black Wolf's grim face peered from the doorway. "You come," he demanded.

Davey shrugged. Tomorrow he would come back. He had to. Where was everyone, anyway?

They pushed off for the peace woman's cabin on the opposite shore where they landed the canoe. Davey stretched his hand to White Wolf, and eyed a large Indian woman lumbering toward them from a bark cabin under an enormous apple tree. Sun-Will-Shine planted her feet in front of Davey, her red shirt billowing. "*Ni quetha*," she said, reaching her strong arms to the two scouts.

"It is our mother," said White Wolf.

Sleepy Indian boys and girls straggled toward her. "*Mettapelou*," she beckoned and they made a circle around her.

Black Wolf jumped to his feet. "Look," he shrieked, throwing the fur he had been sewing onto the hard clay. "It is from the panther." He pounded his chest and grabbed Davey's hair.

Davey stifled a yell.

"I captured this *skillewaythetha* running along the river."

The children laughed and chattered.

Sun-Will-Shine raised her hand to quiet them.

White Wolf had kept back some furs for his mother and pointed to the pile at her feet. "These are skins of red deer, cinnamon bear, and black panther. Moneto gave us good hunting." He glanced at Davey, questioning with his kind eyes if he understood.

Davey nodded. He felt bewildered by the quick motions of the braves, the unfamiliar bare skin, the fresh-killed animal smells.

"This white boy is my friend," White Wolf continued. "He helped me with buzzard down when I cut my leg." He held up one leg, hopping to keep balance. "Just like Shawnee." He pulled Davey toward the peace woman.

A smile cracked her leathery face. She grasped Davey's neck with her calloused brown hand and pushed him toward her hut, then nudged him through the low doorway into a large room with a fire in the center.

"Wait," Davey protested.

But she seemed to have the strength of a buffalo as she stripped him, threw his dirty clothes in a pile, and pushed him toward a wooden tub of water she had heated over the fire.

Davey couldn't get loose. How could a woman be strong enough to do this to him? But she smiled broadly. Perhaps she just seemed stronger than his ma, because he didn't know what was to happen to him next.

All the little Indians had followed the peace woman to her hut, giggling and clapping their hands, and now peered through the holes that were windows. Black Wolf led the mocking, sticking his thumbs in his ears and wiggling his fingers at Davey.

Sun-Will-Shine paid no attention to her mischievous son, and scrubbed Davey's back until it tingled like needles and pins. His long legs and arms stuck out like a turtle on its back. She pulled him out and rubbed him till his skin turned red as apples.

He blushed when she shoved a clean doeskin shirt at him. It all happened too fast for Davey to think much of his own ma and the times she made him and Michael take baths in the round tub next to their cabin. First Michael would pour for him. Then Davey'd dump the tub, and pour steaming water from a fresh kettle for his little brother. It seemed so long ago.

Now, bowls of juicy squirrel meat sat on a mat in front of the fire. The hut seemed more friendly now in the red fire glow. As he sat next to the mat, Davey could see into a small room where Sun-Will-Shine had spread her blanket on the floor beneath a shelf holding a copper pot, a clay bowl, and a spoon made from a shell. There was a doorway next to that, but it was closed off by buckskin. Glancing at the two Indian boys seated next to him, he thought he must look more like them than the white American boy he was, with his suntanned skin and slick wet hair pulled back and getting longer than Ma had wanted it.

"Are you hungry?" asked White Wolf.

Davey had forgotten to be hungry, but now the strong smell and hours without food put such a cramp in his stomach, he stuffed the morsels into his mouth and licked his fingers. "My stomach is full." He tilted the bowl to his lips to drain it.

"We are brothers now," said White Wolf.

Black Wolf sulked in the corner.

Davey smiled at White Wolf, but sadness tugged at his throat again. This might be the Indian brother he had always hoped for. But was he a prisoner? He wanted his own brother. Where was he? He couldn't waste any more time.

"You come." White Wolf motioned his new friend to follow him to the rectangular council house on the hill behind Sun-Will-Shine's bark hut. It stood, sturdily built of wood covered with bark, overlooking the great Maumee River and the rich brown cornfields waiting for seeds to sprout.

White Wolf shouldered past the flap of fur at the entrance. The chiefs from other tribes sat in a circle, a tomahawk thrust in the pole at the center of the council house. Blue Jacket, the strong, pale-faced warrior chief, spoke to the other chiefs. "We are taking too many scalps," he said, his voice low.

Davey had expected a loud, deep voice from this chief who was so much lighter than the other Indians. Ever since Davey had come to Lake Erie territory with his ma and pa he'd heard tales of Blue Jacket's bravery as warrior chief. He wanted to ask him about Michael, but Davey was a little afraid of the awesome chief and anyway this didn't seem like a good time to do that. He wondered why the other chiefs looked so glum smoking their fragrant tobacco.

"He's telling them to be patient, to remain peaceful even if the whites plunder our villages," said White Wolf.

"Don't they want peace?" asked Davey.

"Peace is not the question. They won't give up the land. And they'll do what they have to, to live freely on it."

Davey remembered his pa telling him how the white folks took the Indians' land down the Ohio River. How they broke their word and even killed the sacred animals that lived peacefully to the south of the great river that divides.

White Wolf was talking. "Do you know how the Indian feels about the land?"

"Not exactly."

"We believe the land belongs to the Great Spirit. That it is to be used and cared for by everyone as needed."

Davey shivered. The chief was looking straight at him. A blue military coat hung from his shoulders. He whispered to a brave and pointed at Davey, but Davey couldn't hear what they said.

"What's he saying, White Wolf? Why is he wearing that military jacket?"

"I think he asks about you. The coat was given to him by the British when they said they would help us in the coming battle with the Americans."

"Is that why they call him Blue Jacket?"

"I do not know why. Some say he wore a blue jacket when he came to join our tribe of Shawnee and the chiefs here called him that since he was a young boy."

Suddenly Black Wolf flung open the fur flap and stood by Davey. "You come. My mother has made a bed for you to sleep."

White Wolf motioned Davey to follow him to the bark cabin. "You are tired. The morning will be soon enough..."

"But my brother ... I must find my brother. Your renegades took him. They killed my ma and pa."

"It was not our people who did this. Our leaders punish such evil deeds. Tomorrow will be time to talk."

Davey followed into a small room where the door had been draped with buckskin. He didn't expect to sleep.

It was morning when the sound of rolling drums woke him from the groggy half-sleep that had finally come. Bright sunlight streaked the hard mud floor by Davey's deerskin bed. It took a moment to remember where he was. By raising up on one elbow and peering out Sun-Will-Shine's window he could see the council house.

The wegiwas dotting the hillside seemed empty, their door flaps whipping the breeze. Then he scanned the river. He saw people lining up along the river — braves, warriors, women with their children. They were all there. Black Wolf was giving them something. Davey grabbed his leggings and pulled them up, hopping on one leg to the door. What were they doing? Just then White Wolf appeared at the cabin door and urged Davey to follow him. "Will you be my real Indian brother?" he asked.

"Sure, I want to, but..." Davey felt suddenly cold; even the sweat from his armpits ran cold down his arms. Everything in him said *run*. "You said you were already my brother. What do you want?"

"If you are to be a true Shawnee you must run the gauntlet." He led Davey down the hill to the river and left him standing in front of the first Indian in line. It was Blue Jacket. Davey stared up at him, trying to keep his body still, but wiped his palms on his leggings over and over. When Blue Jacket smiled at him, Davey smiled back and nodded yes. The spirit of the great man had empowered him.

Then suddenly from behind, Black Wolf pushed him. Davey hurtled down the line, branches cutting like whips into his back from left and right. Blood trickled from the welts stinging like bees. He fell on his knees and gritted his teeth. If that's the way they want it, he thought, and got up, squaring his shoulders and leaning back for balance. Someone pushed him from behind again. Hands too far back to break his fall, landed on his face, scraping his skin against the stone.

Children took turns hitting him with sticks. He heard babies screaming, as if they knew something was wrong. Women swatted him with delight. One plump woman tore his leggings and whipped his legs. Davey's shoulder was swelling, but he was on his feet again. He felt his lip, puffy like a blister. Maybe this was his punishment for not saving Ma and Pa, he thought. The line seemed endless, hazy, until finally he fell and couldn't get up. Images ran together as someone lifted and carried him to the peace woman's hut.

In and out of consciousness, he lay on the deerskin. "My brother — I should look for my brother," he whispered. A hand steadied him, sending a sharp pain where his shoulder swelled. He fell back, sinking into dark sleep.

Sun-Will-Shine's minor chant mixed with burning herbs and oils. When Davey finally awoke and sat up, smoke from the fire had cleared and a fragrant odor filled the hut. Sun streamed through the window in the peace woman's hut. The floor blurred when he tried to stand.

Green sprouts of corn lined the fields where only rich brown earth had been when Davey ran the gauntlet. Scars stood out on his arms and legs like the brands he had seen on traders' horses. How could the people he had admired do this, he wondered? But over these weeks, he had survived. He felt stronger, not scared as he was when he hid in the tree hollow. He felt strong enough to conquer anything. What could be worse than this, he thought? He flexed his muscles. He could find his brother now.

The next day White Wolf came for Davey. They went to the Chief's wegiwa where White Wolf left them alone. They sat together, legs crossed on the hard ground.

Blue Jacket stared at Davey for a long time almost fondly, as if he knew him. He drew on his pipe and weighed each of his solemn words. "You have proved to us your strength. You have survived the whipping gauntlet that all braves must survive to become members of our tribe. You were kind to our brave scout, White Wolf."

He hung a sinew necklace with a claw dangling from it around Davey's neck. "Seapessee is your new name," he said. "It means Leaper.

Thinking about the gauntlet, Davey didn't know whether to feel proud or angry. But the sharp claw around his neck reminded him that now he was a member of a new family. It made him feel important, more like the Indians he had always admired. He glanced up at Blue Jacket not sure if he should speak. "My brother Michael was captured by renegades," he blurted. "I have to find him!"

Swiftly Blue Jacket was on his feet standing over him. "Do you think he is here with us?" He sounded impatient. "We do not allow renegades, as you call them. We punish our own for these deeds."

"He might be kept somewhere," Davey insisted. "I haven't even looked across the river at the traders' post yet."

"He is not here. White Wolf is your brother now." He turned sharply and left on soft moccasins.

Davey didn't want to offend the chief, but why shouldn't he ask about Michael? He could look for him all by himself. Yet did he have a choice? In his heart he wasn't sure.

3
✛
White Boy

Early the next morning Davey got up from his deerskin in the wegiwa the tribe had built for him, and went out to watch the sun rise red over the swelling rivers. His muscles felt bigger, firmer, as he squeezed his fists, then grabbed his skinning knife from his leggings. He stared at the strong waters surging past the village toward Lake Erie, and felt life pulsing through his veins. Could he ever make up for not saving his ma and pa? Maybe he needed to stay with the Indians to make him brave. But was it the best thing for Michael? It was a big decision. Ma and Pa were gone and he had nowhere else to go. Ironside lived at the traders' village, but he was never there. No one else knew him or cared what happened to him. At least the Shawnees wanted him.

He needed a map so that wherever he went he could trace his way back. With one leap he skinnied up the elm tree and slit the bark where the branches started. Sliding down, he drew his knife along the side to make a long cut. At the bottom, he lifted the bark from around the tree and carved the lines for rivers, forks, and woods.

He could smell bear oil frying the peace woman's griddle cakes—corn meal, sour milk, and flour. She kept a pewter pitcher full of molasses made from the sugar maple trees. Davey's empty stomach growled, but he stayed by himself, not wanting to intrude unless asked. Ma had taught him good manners.

"I see you make the *ou-ecawteke*, a good map," said White Wolf, crouching next to him.

Davey noticed that White Wolf's eyes were blue, just like Michael's. Suddenly the morning silence was broken by a child's screams. Davey dropped his knife and slid down the bank where a woman was dipping her child in the cold running river. "Don't do that," he shouted.

The swarthy Black Wolf laughed, rolling around on the hill and holding his sides.

"It is all right, Davey," said White Wolf. "The mother punishes her child for something he did."

"I will never understand your customs," said Davey. He scanned the flatland behind the hut. An Indian mother was hanging her baby from a tree limb.

"Mothers make the cradle board soft with mashed bark and animal fur. Then they hang the baby from a tree and wash clothes in river."

The baby's arms were left free so that he could suck a leather pouch filled with sweet maple sugar that seeped through the stitches of the bag.

Giggling girls pretended a buffalo leg wrapped in a blanket was their child. Black Wolf ran after them, taunting with wild screams and yells.

"Davey, it is a bad time to look for your brother," said White Wolf. "Soon the battles will begin again."

"All the more reason to find him."

"Did you know there is a white boy in the fur traders' camp?"

"Why didn't you tell me ...? How long has he been there?"

"I heard this morning from scouts who came in from the south."

"Is it ...?"

"I do not know."

Davey jumped to his feet and ran for the shore. His canoe hit the other bank and lodged in the silt. Up the hill he climbed, puffing with expectation. Sweet applewood smoke curled from Ironside's chimney. Halfway there he heard a high-pitched voice. A short figure ran toward him, then slammed his chunky body into Davey's. "Michael, is it you?"

"Are you an Indian?" The child's voice was low. It wasn't Michael.

Davey lowered him sadly to the ground. "I'm sorry. I thought you were someone else." He put his hand on the boy's shoulder. "I guess that's what I am, an Indian. And you? What are you doing here?"

"You don't look much like a Indian." He examined Davey's doeskin and fingered the claw hanging from his neck.

Davey laughed. He realized he didn't feel much like an Indian either.

"I was captured by some bad Indians," the young boy went on, "and sold to the fur traders. It ain't so bad. Polly's here. She takes care of me. My ma and pa were killed a long time ago."

He was so young. But so was Michael. He had to find him. He left the boy and trudged up the hill to Ironside's cabin.

The tall bulky man filled the doorway. "Davey, I heard rumors about your folks from the Wyandots downriver." He swiped his gray-stubble whiskers with the back of his big hand after a spit to a copper spittoon. "I was up north when it happened. I'm sorry. They were good people. It's a grave loss to me, too." He sat at his crude desk, his face resting in his rugged hands. "What's this about you being an Injun'?"

"I went through the gauntlet, and Chief Blue Jacket says I'm one of them now. Mr. Ironside, you were a good friend to Pa. Could you help me find Michael?"

"Michael's missing? How long's he been gone? You know about the war heatin' up, Davey? We've been up north talkin' to the British agents about our fur trade routes."

Davey slid into the Windsor chair across from Ironside. He could see through a low doorway to another room where a mattress was on the floor. He hung his head and studied the wood boards. He couldn't answer Ironside's questions. He wasn't sure how long Michael had been gone, but the fields were striped with corn shoots now, so it must be May or June. And with the war coming, it would be more complicated to find Michael than he had thought.

"Don't give up, son. We'll think of something." Ironside drummed his fingers on the table. "Old Simon Girty, the British spy, might be the ticket." His dirt-lined fingernails ticked on the table. "No. He's too weasely. Before you know it he'd have Michael sold right back to the Indians."

"What about the other one — Mr. Moore? Pa said he's a friend of yours."

"I'll talk to him. He might know where to look."

"That little boy said something about Polly. Can I go see her?"

"Polly Meadows? I don't know what help she'd be. Washes clothes for the Indians who captured her in a battle down south." He rested his pipe on the table, his deep set eyes, nested in wrinkles, darted with thoughts. "Sure, maybe she knows something."

Davey thanked Ironside and headed for Polly's cabin, when a sound like thunder came from across the river. Horses' hooves were stirring clouds of dust along the bank. White Wolf was waving his arms in the air, signaling Davey to come. There was no time for Polly now. He ran for the canoe and paddled fast to the Indian shore.

Mellow sun lit the sky with a white light. At the council house Blue Jacket hurled himself from his black stallion. "Someone told the American general, Anthony Wayne, we were coming to Fort Recovery to fight him!" He walloped his horse on the rump, sending it to be rubbed down. "Two thousand Lake Indians attacked Fort Recovery while we, the great Shawnee nation from the confluence of the Maumee and Auglaize Rivers, were preparing to meet with Wayne for a peaceful exchange of prisoners. When we arrived, General Wayne thought we were part of the attack instead of a peaceful mission."

Davey remembered his pa talking about Anthony Wayne, the American general. "My pa said Anthony Wayne was going after the British to push them off our territory, not to fight with the Indians."

"They shot at us." Sweat dripped from Blue Jacket's black hair. "They attacked us, caught us off guard, we had to escape."

Davey followed White Wolf and other young braves

crowding around the fur flap of the council house to listen. Black Wolf shoved Davey's shoulder. Davey pushed him away. The dark scout was already smeared with war paint.

"Wayne is coming after us from the south," the chief announced. "The war has started. Our people are becoming angry because of so many broken promises by the Americans. The American generals have said they will take only the land we agree to sell them. Now they say it is not our land to sell and they take more. They do not keep their agreements. Even young Shawnee scout, Tecumseh, has witnessed his father's death at the hands of the Americans when he was seeking peace with them."

The chiefs who had assembled in the council house nodded agreement, except Miami Chief Little Turtle. "The Americans are led by a chief who never sleeps, this General Anthony Wayne," said the old man seated next to Blue Jacket. "We should listen to the spirit who whispers to us to make peace."

"I, too, want peace," said Blue Jacket. "But the Americans will kill us if we don't fight now. My scouts tell me that British officers are on they way down the Detroit River from Canada. They will help us. When they cross the western side of Lake Erie and come up the Maumee River to the big rapids, they plan to use the old fort there." He drew lines in the clay with a sharp stick.

"The fort is here." He stabbed the earth. "Here on the south bank of the Maumee." He marked the river running past the Shawnee village through the rapids toward Lake Erie. "McKee's place is just a mile from the abandoned fort near the rapids. Colonel McKee, the British spy, has supplied us with British weapons before. We will make camp with him. Then the British can give us ammunition when the Americans attack."

Davey's eyes never left Blue Jacket. Now he was more worried about Michael than ever. There might not be time to search for him before Wayne attacked. Suddenly, without thinking, he interrupted the chiefs in their council. He called out from the rear of the room. "Wasn't the war with the British over a long time ago?" Forgetting his fear, he muscled in closer to the chiefs. "Why are the Americans fighting the British now?"

Silence was so think even the old men seemed to stop breathing.

Quickly Blue Jacket stood. "Seapessee, follow me." He hustled Davey out of the building.

The flickering fire danced across Davey's face as he sat with Blue Jacket and his graceful wife, Wabethe, in their wegiwa. His eyes watered from the yellow flames in the center of the tent.

Blue Jacket gathered his beautiful wife into his muscular arms. "Wife, I love you." He looked at Davey. "I have written many peace letters to the Americans."

Davey wondered how this civilized man, who spoke English and could read and write, became chief of an Indian tribe. Someday he would ask him. Now he would listen.

"I have offered peace over and over. They do not listen."

"Could the British be intercepting your peace letters to the Americans?" Davey asked without shyness.

"I suppose they could." Blue Jacket poked the fire till the flames shot up. "They have much to gain from our disagreements with the Americans."

Davey watched Wabethe walk over to lower the flaps.

The powerful chief pulled Davey aside and whispered, "When the time comes to leave for the rapids, I will tell Wabethe to take the women and children to the hills to hide from Wayne."

Blue Jacket put his hands behind his head and rested on the woven blanket. "The fighting here by the great lake never stopped," he began, answering Davey's question about the British. "The British retreated to Canada after the big war, but they still believed they could have fur trade and colonies if they used Indians to fight the Americans." His eyes flashed like fired steel. "*We* only wanted our hunting lands." He stared at the top of the wegiwa. "We will do anything to keep them."

Davey wasn't listening any more. With everyone fighting, he wondered only how he'd ever find his brother. He jumped to his feet and hurled the words at Blue Jacket. "You don't know what it's like to have a brother one day and the next day you don't know where he is, or what's happened to him. My ma said we'd take care of each other. No matter what happened, we'd stick together. I lost my brother. I have to find him. I want to leave, Blue Jacket. I have to leave."

Slowly the powerful chief sat up. "Are you not our brother now? We need every man to fight the battle. I understand your concern for Michael. But it is too late for you to go alone. You will be caught by Americans if you stand up for our people. If you don't stand up for our people, you will be caught by the Indians. I know the sadness in your heart. These have been my secrets too."

Davey thought he saw tears filling the strong man's blue eyes, but he was thinking about his own problems. Would he really be a coward to stay, or a fool to go? What was bravery, anyway? What was the best way to find

Michael? He heard the chief's voice quietly breaking through his own confusion.

"Maybe you will find another way," he said.

4

+

Polly

Davey couldn't get Polly off his mind. He had to see her. He crossed the river before sunrise and went right to her cabin next to Ironside's. He peered through the open door.

Polly Meadows was packing her red embroidered carpet bag, stuffing stockings, green slippers, a purple roundabout and pink pantaloons into the bag. She held a creamy-colored doeskin pullover to her ample bosom, admiring it in the cracked mirror hanging on the log wall.

"May I come in?"

Quickly she moved to her basket of laundry when she saw Davey. "Whew," she exclaimed, tossing the doeskin to her bed, "I never seen so much dirt."

"May I come in?" Davey repeated. "I'm..."

"I know who you are. That white orphan turned Indian." She eased her plump body into a chair.

"I want to know if you've heard anything about my brother."

Polly swiped a damp towel and threw it to the basket

for drying. "I know spies are all around here — British spies, American scouts, French traders." Davey hurled the words with desperation. "Somebody's got to know something!"

Polly put a finger on her chin. "You find me a way to get loose of these bloody savages, I'll go huntin' fer him myself. But shy of that, there's nothin' I know, and nothin' I can do!"

"Looks to me like you were already plannin' to go somewhere." He strode from the cabin and knocked on Ironside's door just a few feet away.

The burly trader, studying a piece of yellowed paper at his desk, looked like he'd been up all night. "You want me to send Polly with Moore down the Maumee to check out the Wyandot village?" He never looked up.

"Can you do that?"

"Polly wants to go east. She's always packin' her things. Maybe Blue Jacket would do you a favor and free her so's she could look for Michael."

"I'll go with her," Davey said with determination. "How can we do it?"

"Well, as I see it, go downriver to the Wyandots. If Michael ain't there, check out the Miami camp. Then go on into Lake Erie." He clenched his pipe between his teeth. "When you find him, take him back east till this war thing settles."

"I have an uncle in the east. His name is Henry." Davey shuddered. "But what if we can't find Michael?"

"Don't think about that. Moore can get you on up to Detroit by canoe along the edge of the lake up the strait. There are three brigs at anchor in Detroit, all good-sized, two hundred tons or more, belonging to his majesty, George the third. My friend, Captain Spears of the British Navy, will let you board one of his vessels and cross Lake Erie to Fort Niagara." Ironside pushed the map away and balanced on the back legs of his chair.

"But if we can't find him, I'll never know if Michael is alive or not, or where he is." Panic raised the pitch of Davey's voice. He clamped his teeth together hard, grinding his jaw. "I'll just do this myself," he muttered.

"Moore knows this territory, Davey." Ironside swung out of his chair and shook Davey's shoulders. "The tribes know him. It might be better for Michael if Moore goes."

"Then I'm going with him," Davey insisted, shrugging off Ironside's hands.

"What's the use of both of you gettin' killed?"

The words hung in the air. Davey was stunned into silence.

"Let Moore take Polly along to care for the boy. You know there's nothin' like a female to care for a young 'un. And maybe if you make a deal with Blue Jacket, tell him you'll stay and fight for him, he'll let Polly go."

Suddenly the door flew open. Simon Girty swaggered in. "They'll never find him," he said, grinning through yellowed teeth. "I just got back from there. They'll never make it past the Wyandots. They're drinkin' and fightin' amongst themselves." His black hair fell in oily streaks across his low forehead. Pistols poked from his belt.

"They'll make it. And they'll find the kid," said Ironside.

Simon threw back his head and sent chilling laughter through the cabin.

A cold shiver raised gooseflesh on Davey's arms.

Ironside put a hairy arm around Davey. "No use going south, Davey. That's where the fighting's started. Wayne's string of forts from Cincinnati to Fort Recovery have been fighting with the Indians all along the way."

Davey brooded. He wondered what was best for Michael.

A flurry of excitement called their attention to the door. The scout, William Moore, had arrived from the south. "The American soldiers are building a bridge out of loose mud and water across the river at Camp Beaver Swamp," he announced. "They're building another fort they call Adams. The Indians captured one of the American quartermasters. The warriors are making him give them Wayne's plans."

Wayne's really coming, thought Davey.

"Never mind that now, Moore." Ironside linked arms with him. "We've got another job for you, my friend."

A short time later, Davey paced outside Blue Jacket's wegiwa. He was still torn about whether to go for Michael. He practiced asking, "Would you free Polly Meadows so she can look for my brother?" That didn't sound right, he thought. He tried again. "I'll stay and fight for you." *No*, he thought, *I'm going myself.*

Blue Jacket pushed the flap aside and stretched his arms above his head. "You have returned to learn my secrets," he said, steering Davey toward the council house on the hill. "We have no time to talk, but I will tell you this part. *I am not an Indian.*"

"What do you mean?" Davey's eyes widened. "Why…"

"I will explain later, when the moons have passed. Now I have many things to prepare." Abruptly he disappeared through the council house door.

Davey forgot to ask about Polly. He longed for Michael. He ached for someone to talk to, to tell these secrets to. Did the chiefs know Blue Jacket wasn't an Indian? Was he a spy? Was he British? Or American?

Davey noticed the sky was turning dark before noon, as low, grey-bellied clouds hung from the horizon. He caught up with White Wolf, who was chipping flint by his mother's hut.

White Wolf cupped his ear. "Listen!"

The silence was eerie, not like the thick velvet silence of August nights, but an absence of noise, as if the earth held its breath. The air was stagnant, coated with a stale musty odor. Every leaf was still. Young corn, soft and milky in the ear, were still as stones.

Davey turned to White Wolf, startled by a deafening crack of thunder. Then sudden wind swayed the massive trees. Rumbling thunder joined the dull boom-boom of Indian drums.

"Hug the ground," shouted White Wolf as a mass of whirling fluid formed a funnel in the blackened sky, and spun toward earth like a giant top.

They huddled in the corner of the square corn patch behind the peace woman's hut. An elm tree bent to the ground, then split apart and crashed just missing the top of Davey's head. Gale winds ripped roofs off, wegiwas flapped in the wind and sailed through the air. The rivers surged and bubbled like boiling water.

"There goes your mother's roof," yelled Davey, poking his head up.

"Stay flat," warned White Wolf.

Davey pressed his cheek against the moldy ground. Pounding rain hammered him down to his bones.

Suddenly, without warning, the sky cleared. The quality of the air had changed. Bright sun spilled onto the earth like liquid gold. The wind stopped. As quickly as the storm had come, it left.

Davey knew what a tornado was but this one had come

up fast, and had left just as fast. When he looked around he saw the whole village wasted, but everyone was bustling around like ants. It was clear to Davey that the Indians were doing more than just cleaning up after a storm.

Children were spinning their tops; boys rolled a hoop down the hill, shooting at it with bows and arrows as it passed by. Young braves lined up at a mark to race, some played stick ball. Others jumped into canoes to fish. Young women pushed off in canoes with a large ball to play lacrosse in the water.

Davey helped Sun-Will-Shine put her cook-pot back and started her fire. He gathered her dresses and blankets strewn across the ground and folded them neatly in a pile. Just then he noticed Black Wolf crouching behind the toppled apple tree next to the roofless hut, and wondered what he was up to.

Davey walked over to White Wolf who had resumed chipping the flint by his mother's fire. "What's going on, White Wolf?" he asked.

He handed Davey a flaking tool—a piece of deer antler wrapped to the tip with buckskin strips—then placed a flint point on a square piece of leather. "Here, *Sacouka*, see?" he said. "Press the piece of horn against the spearhead. This is how I attach it to the foreshaft of my spear." He picked up another flint and split it with one blow of his hammer stone, hit it on the edges over and over, then with one quick stroke chipped the brittle flint away.

"What's going on, White Wolf?" Davey pressed his question.

White Wolf looked at Davey with his crystal blue eyes. "It is time for the Corn Feast. Deep summer will be here

soon. Now that corn is soft and milky in the ear, we make
feast to Moneto."

The summer sky seemed more brilliant to Davey, as if
the storm had flushed everything out. Blue Jacket knelt
by the river pointing his hands heavenward. Davey could
hear his chant.

"Thank you, Moneto, for the butternut bark and yellow poplar root," he sang. "For blood root, wild ginger,
crawfoot beech and wild cherry, white ash roots that save
us from the snake." He ended the trembling melody and
lowered his body into the river.

Soon Blue Jacket leaped from the cold water and
climbed the bank toward Davey. "Join your brothers in
the moccasin game, Seapessee," he called.

"How can they play games when you must go to
battle?"

Blue Jacket frowned. "It is good for them to laugh and
play the games of dice with button horn, and to wrestle
and run to get rid of the energy."

A sudden feeling spread over Davey. It was a new feeling, as if he understood Blue Jacket; as if he could be-
long here with these people. He remembered Polly, but
he needed to be sure what was best for Michael. "I would
rather wait here with you, Blue Jacket."

The chief nodded. "There are those of us who carry
the burden. It will be so with you, *neaqueytha*, my son."

Davey smelled wild turkey cooking in dry herbs over
the hickory coals. White smoke billowed in the Azure sky
from Sun-Will-Shine's roofless cabin. He stayed with
Blue Jacket, eating creamy corn pudding from husks.

"You are sad, Davey."

"I was thinking of Ma." Now at last was the time Davey
had waited for, and he was ready. "Chief Blue Jacket, I

must ask you a favor. Would you free the prisoner Polly
Meadows so she can look for my brother? I will stay and
go to battle with you."

A smile traced across the chief's lips. "I said you would
find another way." Blue Jacket called a young scout to his
side. "Free the white woman, Polly Meadows," he commanded, clamping his strong hand firmly around
Davey's neck. "And so it is done, my son."

"Thank you," said Davey. Now he knew why he had the
new feelings. It was his pa. Blue Jacket was like his pa—
kind, firm, caring. And he knew somehow this strong
man would be there for him when he needed him.
Quietly, almost so the great chief couldn't hear, he whispered, "my father."

Wabethe moved gracefully toward them, her long
skirt bound with fluttering purple and pink ribbons. Her
black hair was parted in the middle and tied behind;
wide silver bracelets clung to her smooth arms. A sweet
aroma rose from the clay pot she carried. "It is for you,
my favorite men," she said, her doe eyes softening.

Davey put his nose close to the dish.

"It is the rich, thick juice from wild grapes, pressed
and heated. Then I add sugar and dumplings when it is
boiling."

He took the horn spoon from Wabethe and let the liquid roll around his mouth, his lips puckering from the
sweet, acid taste.

Wabethe took Davey's hand and led him to a circle of
couples dancing around a fire. Joining in to the beat of
drums and the low chant, they alternated couples, two-
by-two, in double file and glided in a serpentine path
around the campgrounds. Wabethe held her arms outstretched at the sides like wings in flight. They were

bending, hopping, swaying, running — toe-heel, toe-heel — trotting, stomping, singing "Yu-wooo, hi! he-hie."

Davey, flushed from excitement, left the shuffling dancers and rested against a young oak tree. Wabethe seemed so kind, so full of life, he thought. Like Ma, only younger. The Corn Feast reminded him of the hay rides when Ma'd bake cakes and drop dumplings into the chicken broth. And Pa'd uncork the cider jugs and he and Michael would hide behind the house and drink it till they got silly. Neighbors would come, and dancing would go on till dark. It was *do-see-doein'* kind of dancing, but it was all the same. Usually the memories stayed in his mind's shadow. Now they flooded in and he swallowed back tears. Pa would wonder about this war coming, thought Davey. "I'm real scared, Pa," he murmured out loud. "And I miss Michael." When he looked up, Black Wolf was watching him.

5

✝

It's Time

Pa would have wanted him to do his share. That's just how Pa was, thought Davey. He might wonder why Davey was choosing to go with the Indians. But if he explained how he felt about the Indians, and how he always wanted to help them, Pa would understand. Davey was sure of that. *Now if I got killed, Pa wouldn't be happy about that. And Ma would ... die herself.* Davey caught himself thinking as if they were still alive. His throat began to feel as if it could squeeze tears right up out of the corners of his eyes. "But dyin's not what I'm intending to do," he said quietly. He straightened. Davey was feeling a lot like Pa himself, older somehow.

A crimson line marked the margin of the morning sky. Sunlight sparked off edges of tomahawks in the Shawnee village.

Blue Jacket handed each warrior a British flint-lock rifle and some ammunition. Davey checked his hard stone hatchet and made sure his gunpowder was dry. Suddenly he realized it was the Americans, his own people, he'd be fighting. For a moment he just stood there, confused.

39

White Wolf poured black powder down his gunbarrel, and made sure the hammer would hit the cap and set the powder on fire as it pushed the bullet out the barrel.

Davey stripped to the waist and smeared his chest with vermilion and yellow paint. He pulled his black hair tight behind his ears and secured it with a circular piece of deer antler. Horn and pouch slung over his shoulder, he swung onto his pony.

White Wolf shrieked, "It's time to go. The hunters have slain twelve deer for the feast tonight. Blue Jacket has raised his tomahawk."

They kicked their ponies into the thundering herd and traveled hard to the wide Maumee River. A trail of smoke from the deserted Shawnee village disappeared. The women had already left their fires.

"The sky's red," Davey said, looking back.

"The sun is just angry." White Wolf galloped after the older warriors.

Davey's little pony couldn't keep up at first, then her strong legs hit stride and to his relief he could see Blue Jacket's black crow feathers bobbing up and down in the distance.

They arrived at McKee's supply post north on the Maumee River and made camp. It was a short distance from the British fort just this side of Lake Erie, where Davey could hear the English soldiers hammering and pounding around the old moat overlooking the river.

Davey jumped from his pony and grabbed Blue Jacket's horse to cool him down. "You're worried, aren't you?" he asked the chief, leading the black stallion in a circle.

"We lost many horses at Fort Recovery, Seapessee, at the hands of the Americans. It is such sadness to me that we fight the Americans. We are not a part of this bitter American-British fight, but we must do what is best for us." The chief raised a pole and drove it into the ground. He attached the skins for a tent. "The scouts have been reporting to me about General Wayne's progress. But our spies can't match Wayne's. We're surrounded by American white eyes. They know everything we do."

"You are much smarter and braver than Anthony Wayne. And anyway, we outnumber them."

But the powerful chief didn't answer. He had settled by his wegiwa and was already dozing.

Davey left his worried chief and led the horses to the river's edge to drink. He saw Black Wolf dart behind a tree.

Davey could feel the dark Mohawk's eyes watching him, but continued brushing the horses, burying his dislike for the bully, Black Wolf.

At dawn voices woke Davey. He poked his friend who was asleep next to him. "You hear something?"

White Wolf shot up from his mat and moved closer to listen. "It's one of our scouts. I think he is wounded."

"Let me see." Davey grabbed his rifle and pulling on his moccasins hopped to Blue Jacket's wegiwa.

The scout was giving his report. "I took the place of my friend. I could see he was bleeding. I couldn't tell if he was dead. They had been asking him questions before they shot him. I think they know we are camped near McKee's supply house.

Davey moved in close to Blue Jacket.

"Wayne knows the British militia came here from Detroit to help us." The reporting scout was breathless. "The Americans think you plan to attack them at the foot of the rapids. They're coming this way now!"

"Wayne's already at Snaketown," another young brave interrupted. "Somebody told him that if he'd stay there for ten more days, Blue Jacket would let him know if we wanted war or peace."

Blue Jacket stiffened. "Get a party together!" he commanded. "Go among the Americans and tell them we want peace." He scribbled a note. "Get this to Wayne."

Davey felt a new pride welling up in his throat. Finally he could do something. He spun around and snatched the letter from Blue Jacket. "I'll take it. I'll make him listen!" he said.

Blue Jacket hesitated. "Seapessee," he said faintly. He studied Davey's eyes, holding him there with his gaze. "Go then," he said. "Take White Wolf with you."

Davey straddled his pony and streaked toward Snaketown with White Wolf. They retraced their steps along the Maumee toward their old village.

Approaching the bushy encampment at Snaketown, just a few miles north of their old village, they slowed their ponies, picking their way carefully so the enemy wouldn't hear the snapping twigs.

The ground was marshy. They rode right into a miniature volcano of swirling gnats. For an instant they were distracted. Slimy green moss stretched to the water. White Wolf's pony slipped. A shot rang out.

As Davey turned to see if White Wolf was hit, a rifle bullet sliced the air in front of his nose. Down went White Wolf's pony. A voice cut the humid air. An American soldier raced toward them.

"The letter, the letter," cried Davey.

"No," said White Wolf. "They think we are spies. Go, go."

Davey squeezed his pony's side as White Wolf swung

up behind him. The pony's sturdy legs tightened and released like coiled springs. Davey could feel pieces of the
bank crumbling under her hooves. He leaned forward.
"You can make it," he urged.

With one courageous effort the pony pulled her legs
from the mud and plunged toward the opposite ledge.
Davey toppled forward, but hung onto her neck. White
Wolf's strong thighs gripped her sides. They landed and
raced the wind for camp.

The next morning, news filled the Indian camp that a
small peace party had been mistaken for spies and one
of the good horses was shot and killed when the party
escaped.

6

✛

Roch de Bout

Davey knew he had failed. His stomach went queasy when he heard another scout tell Blue Jacket that Wayne was at the rapids. If only he had reached Wayne with the letter before he was discovered and fired on.

Black Wolf appeared out of nowhere, like a panther stealthily padding through dark woods. "You have spoiled our chances. You are not Indian!" he said.

Davey glared at him. He was an Indian now, even if Black Wolf made him feel uncertain. *I'll prove it,* he thought. He left his wegiwa and moved cat-like along the river until he could see the American soldiers through thick green vines over the crest of the bank. They had thrown up barracks, long thin wood shacks, and were storing baggage and supplies there.

Davey moved closer. He heard a thin-voiced soldier call the place Fort Deposit. Resting his rifle muzzle in the low crotch of a bush, Davey held his breath and listened. The soldiers were planning to attack early in the morning. "It may be a date to remember," one of them said. "August 20, 1794." Davey heard it with amazement.

Davey lay flat in the weeds as the hours inched by. At dust he returned unseen to the Shawnee encampment and reported immediately to Blue Jacket. "Their camp is just opposite that rocky island they call Roch de Bout. They're talking about attacking us in the morning."

"We must plan our own attack and go silently tonight to Roch de Bout," said Blue Jacket.

In the eerie twilight, Davey and White Wolf followed the Indian band toward Roch de Bout. They never got to the island. They ran straight into American troops who seemed so scared of the painted Indians, they took off before any shots were fired.

The band of Shawnees stayed in the tall grass through the night, listening and waiting for the American troops to return. In the quiet hours before dawn Davey heard Wayne's legion marching toward the empty Indian camp near the British stockade. At the same time, another group on horseback thundered along the opposite bank of the Maumee River. It must be Wayne's cavalry, Davey thought.

Breathless, a scout announced that the infantry was in the woods west of the hill where they had stayed during the night. He reported that they passed him heading north toward the place where Wayne thought the Indians had set up camp.

"It appears Wayne comes in a central direction," said Blue Jacket. "He does not plan to attack on the island of Roch de Bout."

"Will we still go there?" asked Davey.

"No, we must change our tactics." At a quick signal from Blue Jacket, the warriors formed a line in front. "Here we will hide our men in ditches in three lines. The lines will stretch for two miles at right angles to the

Maumee River. Our strength will be in front, hiding in the tall grass."

Suddenly Davey saw Wayne's rag-tag volunteers approaching Blue Jacket's front line. "The Americans are coming," warned Davey.

The Indian front line all fired at once, forcing the men to retreat. Davey didn't have a chance to fire his rifle. He settled in a ditch in the thick brush, pulling his pony down in the tall grass beside him. His heart slammed against his chest. He could feel Blue Jacket's shoulder to his right, and White Wolf's hot breath on his left arm.

"Follow me!" said Blue Jacket.

Wayne's volunteers were running backwards, breaking up the solid line of regular troops. "Look, they're going through the front guard of regulars." Davey laughed.

"Get back in the high grass," called Blue Jacket.

"They're falling in with the infantry to our right," Davey said in disbelief. He stood gaping at the confusion among the American troops.

"Seapessee, get down." Blue Jacket's voice was almost lost in the rattle of rifles. "They'll see you. Get down."

Davey reeled and dropped to his knees.

The American soldiers seemed too confused to notice. Indians outnumbered the whites, but the Americans were coming from everywhere.

Davey moved out. Today he would show his bravery, then he could make the hurting go away. Blue Jacket grabbed his arm and pulled him down. The light infantry company moved over to join a horse brigade to the left of Davey. "Let me see," said Davey. "They're pulling back. Are they retreating?"

"No, they're just tightening ranks to make a solid front."

"Do not worry, Davey," whispered White Wolf. "Blue Jacket will lead us. And we have the British help." White Wolf tried to touch Davey but couldn't reach him. "Moneto keep you safe," he said.

Davey looked into White Wolf's eyes. He remembered something Pa had told him about how a gentle man was a gentleman. White Wolf was like that. "You scared?" Davey asked.

"A little," said White Wolf.

"You're lucky you still have your ma," said Davey.

"We'll be brothers forever," said White Wolf.

By now Davey was more interested in watching the legion passing the battalion of riflemen.

Suddenly a charge rang out. General Wayne's right column came up firing. A shot ricocheted and Chief Turkey Foot fell. Shock seemed to stun Blue Jacket. His friend had fallen. He hurtled onto his stallion. Davey followed.

"Come up behind the Americans," shouted Blue Jacket, his jaw set like granite.

Davey clamped his knees to his pony's sides, tucked his toes beneath her belly and placed his hand next to the mane. He turned and cut the wind, his pony stretching her short legs as far as they would go. He left Blue Jacket and rode directly to the British Fort.

"Somebody, come, listen to me," Davey shouted as he swung from his pony and pounded the gate. But no one answered. The gates remained shut.

He leaped onto his pony's back and rode hard to McKee's supply house. "Colonel McKee, we need help, now! We need cannons, more guns, men..." His voice fell. No one answered. All the British promises of help—broken. Why? There wasn't time to think now. Instantly, Davey urged his pony forward to tell Blue Jacket that no help was coming. He ran into a retreating band of Indians.

Shots sprayed all around him. Indians were running, stabbing, shooting wildly. They were falling everywhere.

Wayne's cavalry had circled the Indians' right flank and attacked from the rear. At the same time his legion with the light infantry attacked from the front. The Indians couldn't get free from their hiding places in the high grass. They tried to retreat to the rapids and escape to the other side, but before reaching the bank they were intercepted by the cavalry, which had been hiding in the woods to the east of the river.

A sea of blood mingled with the waters of the Maumee. Terror froze Davey. He jumped from his pony and dropped his rifle in a din of choking screams.

The blade of a bayonet slit the side of an Indian standing next to him. "White Wolf," he shrieked, "my brother!" Davey bent down to lift White Wolf's head when another American soldier stormed up to him waving his bayonet wildly.

In a split second Davey straightened. His rifle was gone, but he still had his skinning knife. He grabbed for the soldier's hair, glassy eyes fixed on him.

Suddenly Black Wolf appeared from behind, seized the soldier's hair out of Davey's grasp, and peeled his scalp away. "Whooaaa!"

The savage grin on Black Wolf's lips chilled Davey's blood. A burst of anger flooded up from his chest. His chance to avenge the murder of his best friend was snatched away from him, just as he got the courage he needed. But was that really bravery? The question flashed through his mind. He felt disgust, his own savage smile frozen on his face. His heart thundered. Maybe he had been saved from an act he would have regretted for the rest of his life. He couldn't be sure of anything. He couldn't breathe. Behind him he heard someone splashing wildly in the river, spewing water, arms swinging wildly in the air. He clenched his fists to fight. A strong arm encircled his chest and whipped him over the front of a horse. It was Blue Jacket.

They made it to the top of the ridge and looked back. A thousand Indians had fallen, scattered at the water's edge and lying twisted among the trees downed by the tornado. Did Black Wolf get away?

"Hie, yee," Blue Jacket screamed and leaped down the bank. Wayne had set fire to the high grass where they were hiding and the hot flames crackled at their backs.

Davey was faint. His chief urged the black stallion forward along the path. They crossed the wide water and just beyond, Davey could see orange sky blazing on the horizon.

Stumbling toward him came the women and children from the hills behind the Shawnee camp. They cried out, "Our homes are gone! They have burned our homes and our fields."

In a flash of memory Davey saw his old cabin burning, his ma lying there. Then she was rocking Michael by the window, the one next to a shimmering spruce tree. It seemed so long ago. He could never move fast enough to save the ones he loved the most. Now White Wolf was gone. He tried to think of the last thing he said to him. He hadn't even said good-bye.

Blue Jacket raised his hand to calm the women,

searching their faces for Wabethe. She pushed past the other women and stumbled toward Blue Jacket's horse. He whipped her onto his stallion behind him. She tightened her arms around his chest and lay her head against his back.

They were both there, Davey and Wabethe, safe on Blue Jacket's horse. They had no home. They had no dream. Davey realized the battle was over and he had no brother, neither White Wolf nor Michael.

7

✝

Swan Creek

Night fell on the wooded area of ancient oak trees. It was higher ground here away from the swamp, and sixty feet up the first branches of the massive live oaks spread out in a canopy over the defeated Indians.

Intermittent bursting shells and crackling fires came from the British fort across the river. The Americans were no longer shooting at the British. They had gone away.

Wabethe put her slender arms around Davey. "My husband cries," she said.

"I cannot cry." He released himself from her arms and found a stick. He tied it to anther stick with sinew and pumped it till warm sparks set milkweed on fire. He tramped down the prairie grass at the foot of a towering oak and made a soft place for Wabethe to sleep.

The warriors were dropping everywhere on the grass, moaning and chanting to sad rolling drums. Two figures carried a litter on their shoulders. They lowered it to the ground. It was White Wolf. Davey fell to his knees.

Sun-Will-Shine moved toward him. Her stony expression gave no clue to the heartbreak Davey knew was inside her.

The sun streaked the sky and met the lingering blazes set by Anthony Wayne in the fields. Women were chewing deer tendons to make screens for the bottoms of the graves.

Davey placed the knife they had whittled together just days ago, beside his brother's body. White Wolf was draped with loose clothing, his black hair lay unbraided against his pale face. Davey wished he could see White Wolf's blue eyes again, but the peace woman had put a heavy cloth over them.

Blue Jacket, Black Snake, and Little Turtle led the procession. Blue Jacket's sad eyes seemed to be searching for the fallen Turkey Foot. Warriors, women and children followed to the narrow grave. They lowered the young, gentle brave and the death chant began.

Davey placed a smooth stone at the foot of the grave and whispered, "Good-bye, *theemcytha*, my brother." Then he turned and ran. Straining every breath, every heartbeat, he could hear Wabethe calling him. "Sun-Will-Shine needs you Davey. She has lost her son." He turned to see Wabethe's small figure standing with Blue Jacket. "Let him go," he heard him say.

Where was he going? He didn't know—just away. He ran from the hole White Wolf lay in and the hole he'd dug for his ma and pa, from the hardness of Indian life, maybe from life itself. The pain of it was unbearable now.

He crossed the wide Maumee River over rocks where the rapids ran shallow. Splashing carelessly with each step of his moccasins, he left the water and climbed the steep hill to the British fort, where he had pounded the gate.

He made his way to the parapet, the huge wooden

wall surrounding the fort. The American soldiers had stopped shooting at the British and had gone away. Indians clustered at the gate, not knowing where else to go, bent over, arms wrapped around their sides and moaning from their wounds. Davey searched the faces for Black Wolf, but couldn't find him. He moved on, striding down the hill, trotting through the woods, and vowing never to trust the British again.

Exhausted, he threw off his blood-stained clothes and lowered his aching body into the cool waters of Swan Creek, letting it roll and slide through the stream. It didn't matter that he'd run away. He climbed the grassy bank and fell asleep.

At dawn's light, a soft, black nose and warm breath brushed his cheek with a familiar nicker. "You found me." He hugged his pony's neck and nestled his head in her thick silver mane. All the pent-up emotions from those years when he thought he was too strong to cry, exploded against the animal's warm hair. Wails and groans bellowed up from deep in his belly. Drenching sobs wracked his body in waves. "Blue Jacket cries," he remembered Wabethe's words.

When his tears were spent, he rode slowly along the riverbank, past the British fort toward the American's deserted Fort Deposit. There was so much to think about. What was he doing there? So much had happened. *Michael's gone. I'm a warrior. My Indian brother is dead. Why was White Wolf taken and not me?* He had watched the tender, brave Blue Jacket suffer when he only wanted peace, abandoned by the British who said they were his friends. What would Davey's ma have said? Would she be proud of him? Would she think he should be on the American side, or be with Michael?

Suddenly he heard a rumbling noise. He dismounted and placed his ear to the ground. The thunder of wagon wheels. He led his pony into a thicket near the bank of Fort Deposit. Just ahead was a dirt road hardly a wagon-wheel wide. Silently he watched from a tangle of brush. It couldn't be Indians; those remaining were back at the fort, still believing the British would protect them. These sounds moved away from the fort. *Seems like Wayne is taking his troops back up the river toward the old Shawnee village,* he thought.

He listened to the clickety-clack rattle down the dirt road. Then he saw them, a cart-load of wounded, bleeding men piled one on top of the other, with spades and axes scattered among them. The bumpy road sent shocks through their bodies. Davey saw a tumble of straw-colored hair, and darted closer. He watched the shadowy forms till they reached a clearing and he had to let them go.

Turning his pony's head to the rapids, he crossed where it was shallow and returned to camp. Blue Jacket was on his horse, leaning down to kiss Wabethe.

"Where are you going?" Davey asked.

"To Detroit, to see why the British closed their doors to us. We need their help for the winter."

"Blue Jacket, I might have seen Michael..." Davey grabbed his sleeve.

"Take our people to Swan Creek. They will be safe there," said the chief, expressionless.

"Chief..."

Blue Jacket swung his stallion into the north wind.

Painfully Davey responded to his chief's command and gave orders to gather roots, berries, and nuts. The women mashed them into fine powder and stored them in deerskin pouches. They ground strips of deer meat and mixed them with animal fat, then scraped and stuffed deer entrails, tied them with sinew and placed the sausages over smoke holes to dry.

It took a few days to prepare the shabby Indians for their new home. Thoughts of White Wolf haunted Davey as he led the long line of Indians away from the sheltering oaks on the afternoon's journey to Swan Creek. He missed Michael and now White Wolf. Could he have done more to save his Indian brother? A rustle of leaves in the shadows pricked his pony's ears. He jerked her to a halt and saw Black Wolf's swarthy face peering at him through the brush. "You think you are savior of my people. You'll see who is leader. It will not be a white boy." Before Davey could answer, Black Wolf disappeared.

The next weeks passed slowly as the band set up camp along the shady creek. Ruby trees of autumn faded into brown. Gloomy light from the pale sun surrounded Blue Jacket as he returned from Detroit. "The British will not help us. I think they were afraid of the Americans, and hid behind their gates. We must find a way to survive," he said.

"White Wolf should be here with us. I should have saved him," said Davey.

"Do not blame yourself, Davey. It is wrong to punish yourself for the past. People we have loved and have loved us in return become a part of us. We carry them with us all the time, even if we no longer see them." Blue Jacket touched Davey's strong shoulder. "Come, I will tell you the rest of my story."

Davey followed him into the square structure of poles and bark, and settle in a corner. A cloud of tobacco smoke filled the hut. Davey glanced at the other chiefs to see if anyone was listening. They were sucking their pipes, eyes closed, their old skin wrinkled in the firelight.

"I told you I am not Indian. I am not even from here. When I was your age, I left my family down by the Ohio River. I went with the Shawnees. My little brother loved me very much. I knew I would miss him."

Davey wondered how he could leave his family like that.

"I'd never thought of the Indians as savages. I had always hunted with the bow as they did, and believed in the rhythm of Nature and the sharing of their people. When the Shawnees adopted me, something inside me said I had come home."

Davey coughed from the smoke. He straightened his leg, asleep under him. The part about leaving his brother stayed on Davey's mind. *No wonder he's treated me special,* he thought. *Maybe I remind him of himself.* Quietly he breathed a prayer, "Please let me find Michael."

"I have lost spirit now," Blue Jacket's eyes were closed.

"Because the Americans won? Or because the British let you down?" asked Davey.

"No, because of the way I lost my little brother. It had been a very long time since I had seen him. It happened shortly before you came to our village..." His eyes widened. "The Americans had a fort along the way from Cincinnati. These Americans were not friends to the Indians. When they attacked, we fought a bloody battle and won."

Blue Jacket continued. "It was then I saw the young boy in the uniform. At first I thought he was just another soldier, but when I heard him call me "brother" I turned around and he was gone. I did not return to search for his body. How I am haunted by his memory." Blue Jacket buried his head in his hands.

Davey shivered. Blue Jacket knew how it felt to lose a brother. *Now he grieves, but once he told me not to blame myself for the past.* Davey wanted to remind him of that, but it was too hard to break the silence. Through the night he stayed with Blue Jacket, rocking back and forth, hugging his knees and he had to consider that Michael might no longer be alive.

8

✝

Decision to Return

As weeks passed and winter nipped at the heels of autumn, Davey kept busy hunting the red fox and white-tailed deer.

Sun patches on the forest floor cheered Davey as he fished through crusts of ice in Swan Creek. He encouraged Wabethe daily that her husband would get stronger after the treaty was signed. But he knew Blue Jacket would never really be the same.

He wrapped himself in a blanket and built a fire, heating a kettle of water and herbs on the icy ground. He pretended to himself that Polly had found Michael and taken him back east. He made up stories about Michael entertaining his cousins with tales of savages burning down their cabin, and about how his other brother, Davey, was probably killed by Indians.

Blue Jacket interrupted his daydreams. Eyes heavy with sadness and disappointment, he leaned over Davey like a curved bow. "They've taken the wounded Americans to a new fort across the Auglaize from our old village, at the place of the traders' camp. They call it Fort Defiance. It is a hospital now."

Davey remembered the cart full of groaning men, clickety-clacking along the dirt road, on that autumn day when he first came to Swan Creek.

"One of the doctors gathered up the wounded soldiers and threw them into a wagon, to take them there," said the chief.

Suddenly Davey remembered the boy with the straw-colored hair bouncing in the wagon. His heart leaped with hope of finding Michael. Quickly he poured steaming herb tea in a buffalo horn for his chief. "How can you be friendly to these Americans we've been fighting?"

"Seapessee! You know there is only one thing I fight for. To me there is only the side of the Indian. But it is a filthy place for a hospital," he went on as if expecting Davey to understand. "Wayne just abandoned it and left rotten trees lying on the ground when they came to Fort Deposit for battle. The traders' village and cornfields are all ashes. I know we have been fighting these men. But the battle is over. The British are not helping us. We will offer what we have to these sick men."

Blue Jacket took a flag of peace and led his band of Indians—chiefs, warriors, women, Sun-Will-Shine, Wabethe, and Davey—through the fields from Swan Creek. Fort Defiance loomed out of the fog on the familiar point dividing the Maumee and Auglaize Rivers. Desolate gray ashes covered the fields where healthy corn had grown. The traders' cabins where Ironside and Polly had lived were gone now, so was the Indian village just across the river.

At dusk Davey spied twenty soldiers on horseback coming toward them along the edge of the Maumee.

The soldiers escorted Davey and the small group of Indians back to Fort Defiance.

Ushered into the mess hall in a long rectangular building inside the fort, Davey sat next to young Andrews, the Surgeon's Mate. Smells of roasted turkey and dressing came from the kitchen. It had been a long time since Davey had smelled onions frying and cranberries bubbling in pots. Eagerly, he grasped the familiar fork and knife to cut his slice of meat. The solemn faces of Indians peered from the benches across the table from the officers.

Savoring the turkey and gravy, Davey asked the Surgeon's Mate about the shots he had heard coming from the fort. "Were you shootin' at someone?"

Andrews passed the steaming rice pudding around. "We punish our soldiers that way, for trying to run away, or for torturing Indians."

"You shoot your own men?" Davey swallowed the lump of stuffing whole.

"Just through the fleshy parts of their behinds. Fifty lashes on the backside in front of the men at evening parade is their usual punishment."

That was one way to do it, thought Davey. "Are the British causin' any trouble?"

"They come down here acting like deserters from the British regiments, but we know who are spies and who are not. Guess they're going to continue this fight even without you Indians."

"I have a favor to ask," said Davey abruptly. "Is there a young boy with curly blond hair among your wounded?"

"Why? Someone you know?" asked Andrews.

"My brother. He's probably too young to be a soldier. He turned nine this winter. But I thought maybe he was around the fightin' and got hurt."

Andrews eyed Davey for the first time, full face. Davey supposed he was wondering how he got to be Indian and all the usual questions.

"I'll check with my men." Andrews picked up on the urgency in Davey's voice and pushed out from the table, then left the dining hall.

Major Hunt, a dignified soldier with silver-streaked black hair, turned to Blue Jacket on his right. He accepted some deer meat and a turkey from the chief, and offered to show him the storehouse.

"We will fill your storehouse with whatever you need," the chief said, bending to whisper in Wabethe's ear. Then Wabethe rose and beckoned the other Indians to follow her.

Blue Jacket motioned Davey to follow him, and Hunt led them to the large log structure across the parade ground.

"Where did all this come from?" Davey waved his hand across the room. Light seeped through the small windows in the storehouse to reveal glasses in boxes; paints; whisky bottles stuck in straw, their cartons ripped open helter-skelter on the hard mud floor; bricks piled up next to the stove; straight-backed chairs climbing to the ceiling, seat on seat; tubs of lard; tea in barrels; bags of onions, potatoes, flour, sugar. "What's this?" he exclaimed, leaning away from a table. A calf's head, raw cut, was ready to be prepared for a meal.

"That's tomorrow's supper." Major Hunt's answer was more emphatic than humorous. "Supplies have been arriving since we set up this hospital right after the battle — the battle of Fallen Timbers we call it."

Davey glanced at Blue Jacket's sad eyes.

"They come mostly from friendly American traders in Detroit," Hunt continued. "Someone they call Ironside, I believe. The medicine he sent helped with the ague fever. That nasty business hit our soldiers right after the battle."

In the corner under tables sat old smudge pots used to help the men breathe. Andrews entered the storehouse, talking. "Stagnant pools of water overflow the meadows in late summer. We think the men inhaled a poison vapor coming from these marshes. Cold fits, then dry hot fits and chills hit them every three days."

"We know this trouble," said Blue Jacket.

Davey examined a wedge of cheese. A tangy smell smacked at his nose as he lifted an apple-barrel lid. It was a smell he remembered from the apple barrel next to the woodpile at home. In late summer Ma took those apples to make cider. They'd heat it when it got frosty outside and Michael would always jump around like it was biting his tongue.

"We can help you with the ague." Blue Jacket gathered his red wearing blanket tighter across this chest.

Davey was sniffing the codfish from Detroit.

"Hosteller's stomach bitters," suggested Major Hunt.

Andrews interrupted. "Peruvian bark is better, sir. Twenty grains of quinine mixed with musilage of gum Arabic." He walked to Davey's barrel and put the lid back on. "The frost seemed to kill the germs in October. The high rivers must have flushed everything out."

It was obvious to Davey they didn't know how to cure the ague.

"We use dogwood bark and purge with calomel and rhubarb," said Blue Jacket.

Hunt glared at the chief, snapped a turn on this

highly polished boots and left the storehouse.
"Davey, I may have found your brother," said Andrews,
sounding apologetic for the Major's rude behavior.
Davey strode from the supply house, Andrews at his
heels. He tramped from blockhouse to field hospital, up
and down the rows of beds looking at the broken,
fevered bodies.

Andrews tried to lead him to the right cot, when
Davey saw the matted straw-colored hair stuck with
blood to a pillow. The boy's face was turned to the rough
wall. Davey leaned down and stared at the empty blue eyes.
It was a very young private. Disappointed once more,
Davey left with Andrews and returned in silence to the
new Shawnee camp on the opposite shore.

9

✟

Bad News

Wabethe caught Davey's arm on his way to his wegiwa. She had been talking to Sun-Will-Shine by the campfire. "Sun-Will-Shine saw her son, Black Wolf, coming from the north all out of breath," she told him. "He whispered to his friends that the Americans are poisoning our food."

Davey sat on a log with Wabethe while Sun-Will-Shine stirred the fire. He was thinking about the dinner he had enjoyed at the fort, wondering if Hunt really trusted them. "I will find out what I can before bothering Blue Jacket with this." He patted her shoulder and crept down the path to the river's edge.

December winds blew against Davey's face as he stood behind a wide oak listening to Black Wolf. The swarthy Mohawk was talking to a small band of braves seated around him in the dark.

"The Americans bait you, my brothers," said Black Wolf. "But soon you will be sick and die from the poison in the food they give us."

Davey knew that any mischief planned by Black Wolf

could upset Blue Jacket's plan to win the friendship of the American soldiers. The wiley scout was planting seeds of distrust among the young braves, so Davey decided to warn the chief. He left the tree and padded through the camp on soft moccasins, but Blue Jacket wasn't there. Davey returned to see what Black Wolf was up to—he couldn't let him start a fight with the soldiers.

It was getting late. A hooting owl made the only sound. Davey knew every inch of ground here on the bank of the Maumee. He had stayed here at the peace woman's hut in the early spring when he had run the gauntlet. Even though the hut was gone, he felt at home on this familiar land. He slid his canoe silently into the river and followed Black Wolf's band of conspirators across the Maumee to the foot of the Americans' new hospital fort.

The fort was surrounded by a think wall of earth. It sloped up toward sharp, pointed pickets twice a man's height that stretched over a deep, wide moat surrounding the fort.

Davey made a mental picture of the four blockhouses at each corner inside the wall. He knew the officers' quarters were in a long rectangular building between them on the Maumee side. Gates were at the north and south. The north gate opened onto a bank of earth. The soldiers could leave the fort by going over the bank to a drawbridge, and crossing the moat to a water-supply ditch that ended in a sand bar on the Auglaize River.

Davey beached his canoe and tracked Black Wolf and his friends as they made their way along the river's edge. He could hear the scheming muffled voices. "We will wait here by the river until soldier guards have gone one time around the fort." Black Wolf's voice rose above the rest. "We will hide on the sandbar. When they start back around to the other side, we will run fast through the water ditch, over the bank and up to the gate. Then...."

Davey could not hear the next words. Ice cakes were forming on the rivers. He shivered as his breath steamed in the frosty air.

The band of five Shawnees tip-toed along the river's edge. It would not be easy for Davey to get away once the Indians had reached the sandbar.

He crouched low until he could see what they were doing. They lit a torch but remained out of sight until the guard soldiers had met and started around to the other side.

Davey's feet skimmed the ground soundlessly as he raced toward the sandbar, coming dangerously close to the heels of the conspirator, Black Wolf. The ill-planning braves were already creeping through the ditch away from their hiding place.

Black Wolf's torch sizzled quietly against the mud. Davey stopped just short of the ditch. Behind him, the Auglaize and Maumee rivers gurgled together. One sound, and the braves would turn and run straight into him.

Davey examined the rivers for escape routes and noticed that the Auglaize running by the old traders' camp was shallower than the Maumee farther down. With a head start, he could wade or swim across and hide there.

Then he realized there were no cabins to hide in. General Wayne had burned them all. He would have to worry about escape later. Now he had to concentrate on saving the American fort and try to keep peace.

He saw the torch go up. Black Wolf had put the fire

brand between the logs supporting the parapet. Just then Davey yelled, "FIRE!" The echo shattered the silence.

"Who goes there?" A soldier's musket clattered.

In the moonlight Davey saw the look of disbelief on Black Wolf's face. He turned and tried to run, his feet like leaden weights. He could hear the thud of moccasins behind him, constant, footbeats against the hard ground. Closer, closer they came. He turned his head.

There was Black Wolf. He had dropped the ashy torch and was springing toward Davey, arms outstretched. They rolled down the path across the sandbar to the edge of the Auglaize. Black Wolf grabbed for his hair. Davey smacked his knee into Black Wolf's side. He screamed. Davey twisted and locked Black Wolf's arms behind him, then Davey heaved him away, turned and dove. When he hit the icy water his legs went numb but he had to keep going. He couldn't look back to see if Black Wolf was coming.

Davey tried to swim, but the ice cakes drifted together now. Teeth chattering and bones aching, he grabbed for the ice, his hand slipping from the shelf. He grabbed again. This time, caught between an ice jam, he held on. With tremendous effort he lifted his leg to the flat surface of the ice and lay there like a dead weight. It swirled around through the black water, bumping ice against ice, and changing its course. Then it broke loose, swirled around to the opposite bank, and lodged in the brush.

Davey didn't care about Black Wolf. He just wanted to be on dry land and get warm. His legs were numb. He tried to pull them out of the water but they wouldn't move. His arms were losing feeling too. The owl moon made eerie shadows on the solid white ice. The night was almost spent. If no one came, he knew he would die there. At least the fort was saved, he thought.

Something rattled through the dead grass above the bank. If he could just stay awake long enough to call for help. But it might be Black Wolf. Terror gripped him again. Then the giant red ball of sun peeked over the trees lining the river. Darkness ebbed and Davey's hope came back.

Eyes peered at him through the vines. Then he saw her. It was Sun-Will-Shine. She was a sight he had thought he would never see again.

The peace woman and the scout who found him dragged Davey's limp body to the shore. Sun-Will-Shine rubbed dewberry root on his bruised legs, then wrapped him in warm buckskin. Just then Davey noticed a shelter about thirty feet from the bank and other rough barracks abandoned by the Americans.

Then he remembered. This was the very place where he and White Wolf had tried to deliver Blue Jacket's peace letter to General Anthony Wayne. Now Davey was here again trying to keep peace, only this time the enemy wasn't General Wayne and the Americans, it was the tribe's own Black Wolf.

The scout built a roaring fire. Sun-Will-Shine massaged Davey's frozen legs. "Blue Jacket will soon return," she said. "He has been in Detroit. Maybe he will bring good news from the British. Maybe they will send provisions for our people."

Davey sighed. "Why can't he understand? The British will never help us."

Later that morning, Davey looked up to see Blue Jacket ride through a clump of trees near the shore. He slid from his horse next to Sun-Will-Shine.

"The British said they will give us nothing if we accept Wayne's treaty. They say we are not fit to fight." Suddenly he noticed Davey stretched out on the blanket. "What are you doing here?"

Davey groaned and raised up on an elbow. "Chief Blue Jacket, the British will never help us. Why do you keep asking them? I think we can trust the Americans to help us now."

"I cannot trust anyone. The Americans have broken their word too many times. I have to do what is best for my Indian brothers." He stood over Davey. "What happened to you?"

Before Davey had a chance to answer, a red-headed private appeared over the snow-coated bank. He tried to look smart but his sleeves and britches sagged with freezing water. Hands shaking, he saluted. "It is Christmas," he stuttered, "Major Hunt wishes to honor your brave white scout at dinner."

"How did they know it was me?"

"They saw you were an Indian and when you yelled *fire* in English, the major thought it was probably you."

Blue Jacket's forehead wrinkled. "What is this about a brave deed, Seapessee?"

The word *brave* jarred Davey. He *had* been brave this time. He had acted. He'd warned the soldiers. Why hadn't he done something like that at the cabin to save his ma and pa?

Before Davey could explain, Black Wolf stormed into their midst on horseback, his eyes flashing black signals to his rebellious friends snaking along behind.

Davey glared at him, clenching his fists. "You have nerve coming here, after what you have done."

"You are the coward, running away through the

river!" Black Wolf crowded the fire, his horse bumping his mother with his rump, and coming to halt before Davey.

Suddenly a round of rifle shots echoed across the frozen landscape. Then another. And another.

Black Wolf whirled his horse around, hooves pawing the air, splaying sparks from the ashes, and charged down the path, his conspirators pounding after him.

Davey jumped to his feet, whipped the rifle from around the soldier's neck and fell to one knee, cocking the barrel. He peered down the muzzle across the Maumee at the sullen grey fort.

"It's a gun salute to the birth of Christ," said the private. "It's for Christmas."

Davey jerked the rifle back and handed it to the soldier, lowering his eyes in embarrassment.

Sun-Will-Shine lifted her shawl around her head and wrapped it securely across her chest. "This, your adopted son, saved the American fort from Black Wolf's mischief."

"Yes. We will cross the river with you," said Blue Jacket, addressing the young private. "The ice should be deeply frozen; the ice cakes have joined together and we will walk across."

They left for the new Shawnee village across from the fort to get Wabethe, and crossed at the forks where the distance was shorter.

At the fort, roasted chicken greeted the band of Indians around the wooden dining table. Wabethe nodded to Davey as Major Hunt addressed him. "Thank you, young man, for alerting our guard and preventing a very serious fire in our foundations." There was a flutter of laughter from the soldiers gathered there for the feast, to which Hunt gave a disapproving stare. He raised a mug of port toward Davey. "I understand you're a white boy. You know both languages, English and Shawnee. We may need you as interpreter for General Wayne's Treaty Council. We would be pleased if you would accept."

Davey glanced at Blue Jacket, who spoke English too. But the Americans didn't know about Blue Jacket being a white man. Davey paused to get his approval. Then he placed his hands on his hips, his feet spread apart and firmly planted. "I have to find my brother first," he said with great authority. "And we will want you to care for our wounded at your hospital. For this I will be your interpreter."

10

✝

Greenville

During the cold month of January, Davey and Blue Jacket carted the rest of the wounded Indians back from Swan Creek to the hospital at Fort Defiance. Black Wolf had disappeared somewhere. They couldn't find him to punish him. Davey wished Sun-Will-Shine could do something about her son. After all, she was the peace woman.

February sugar weather arrived, with false spring freshness breathing around the tips of bare trees. Winter birds chirped. The Maumee swelled as the sun melted snow and broke up the ice. Davey waited, but still there was no word of Michael from the searching expeditions sent by Major Hunt through the northern territory. No one knew about Polly or Moore. And word from Ironside said only that he had sent them on their way, just as he promised.

From his wegiwa, Davey heard a terrible noise. It was like moaning smothered beneath the ice, in deep water where it still ran. After the agonizing sounds, Davey stood on the bank where he had first met Sun-Will-Shine and watched the great river heave up gigantic slabs of ice. They fell on one another forming church-shaped structures like Davey remember seeing in the east.

As February melted into March, Davey dripped sap from a sugar maple into his bark mocock — a container like a sack tied around the tree — then poured it into a brass kettle to evaporate it. He was part of a band of one hundred fifty Shawnees tapping six hundred trees for miles up and down the Maumee, and boiling sap to make syrup and brown sugar.

By April the Indians no longer hoped for British support. But Davey had heard Major Hunt tell them that President Washington would have supplies there for them by spring.

It rained every day in May and still the supplies had not arrived. "Our Miami chief, Naag-oh-guang-ogh, is too wise for the Americans when they promise more butter for our bread. Even this wise chief knows who are to blame for our suffering. They asked too much in their first treaties," said Blue Jacket.

Davey folded his arms across his chest and stood tall. "We must listen to Wayne. We have no choice."

"Yes, we will listen, Seapessee. We will accept American help until we have grown corn."

Indian tribes gathered at the rivers. Blue Jacket had sent for them to attend Wayne's treaty council. Blue cornflowers sprinkled the fields, scattered among white daisies and clumps of orange day-lilies. Davey loved this land. His heart sang with the birds. Hope sprang up in him like the straight green rows of tender corn he had helped plant for the American soldiers. It would be perfect, he thought, if only Michael were there.

It had been more than a year since Davey had seen

Michael. Would his own brother even know him? He wondered if Michael had changed much since those days when they played around the cabin. Sometimes he had gotten tired of his always following him around. Now he just wished he could see him again. If he were still alive, maybe he got with friendly Indians too, he thought. Maybe they were kind to him, Davey hoped.

Blue Jacket had changed during the past months. He was quiet, Davey thought, and the fire had gone out of his eyes. Davey realized he himself had changed too. He was no longer the scared boy, hiding in the sycamore, but more like his own pa. He thought he knew what it was to be brave.

Now, Davey was growing impatient. He had been waiting for a month for Blue Jacket to tell him what he planned to do. He still wanted to keep the sweet river land for the Shawnees. Did Blue Jacket plan to make another treaty with the great white fathers? Or would he fight for the land again?

The day finally arrived, blistering hot and without a breeze. Again the Moon When All Things Ripen had come around. Blue Jacket paced up and down the Maumee bank, then strode to the Council House on the hill.

"We will go to Greenville for the treaty council with General Anthony Wayne," he announced to the tribes assembled before him. Suddenly, Blue Jacket grabbed Davey's shoulder and slowly lowered himself to a bench. "The Potawatomies will leave their women here with ours," he continued. "Wabethe and Sun-Will-Shine will take care of them."

On the following day a long *peroque,* bigger than an ordinary birchbark canoe, was ready at low river. Davey

helped Blue Jacket board the boat and waved goodbye
to Wabethe and Sun-Will-Shine.

"*Pasquemei.*" Black Wolf ran through the village mut-
tering and swatting a swarm of mosquitoes.

After they were settle in the boat, Davey noticed Blue
Jacket's neck was swollen. "You're shaking," he said lay-
ing his cool hand on the chief's burning face. He tucked
a brown blanket around his shoulders. *Cold and hot fits.*
He remembered Major Hunt's description of the sick-
ness at the hospital fort.

River water lapped the sides as a line of Indians,
hunched over and oily with sweat, paddled the long boat
down the river.

By mid-afternoon, they landed at the forks of the St.
Mary's and St. Joe Rivers where Wayne was building a
new fort. A soldier waved his rifle in welcome. "You got
a sick injun' on board?"

"It's our chief. He's got ague."

The young soldier ran to meet them, putting his arm
around Blue Jacket and carrying him to an isolated tent.
Davey slipped his blanket under the chief's head and
ran for water. He heard the soldiers talking. "Chiefs
Buckangehela, Peke-telemund and Teleboxti have already gone to Greenville with three hundred Indians.
Chief Tarhe took a hundred eighty Wyandots down the
rapids."

Davey wished he could tell Blue Jacket that his friend,
Black Snake, took a hundred forty-three Shawnees, just
as he had asked him to. And Little Turtle took seventy-
three Miamis. But his chief was too sick from the swamp
fever to hear.

Chiefs New Corn, Asimethe and Sun took two hundred forty braves, and the Chippewas, Ottawas, Weas,

Kickapoos, Piankeshaws and Kaskaskias had all gone to Greenville. The rest of the Shawnees who had accompanied Blue Jacket and Davey had already left Fort Wayne for the treaty council.

July sun burned a hole in the sky on the day Blue Jacket tried to stand. "My son," he whispered.

Davey lifted a tin cup to Blue Jacket's thin lips "Red Pole arrived at Greenville today. He took a hundred and forty Shawnees with him."

"Good" he said, and tried to stand again.

"Sit down," said Davey. "You are still too weak. I haven't told you Anthony Wayne has asked to see you when you are well."

"Let me see him now. Bring me my horse."

"I will. But first let me help you dress." Davey brought the white shirt Wabethe had packed, with wide pleated yoke and buttoned opening down the center. Loose purple ribbons fluttered across the back. The arms were wide. Dark blue, light blue and yellow yarn was woven in a sash. Blue Jacket slipped wide silver armbands around his weakened muscles and flexed them to test his strength.

"Here is your blue silk scarf." Davey placed it around his neck with a choker necklace of bone and glass.

"Davey, is it true one of the women at our village is dead? The scouts do not know who it is."

Davey continued to drape a purple bandolier over his left shoulder, crossing it over the chief's heart and over a bright red wearing blanket. A purple turban wound around his head with a black ostrich feather stuck in the back.

Their eyes met. Davey knew Blue Jacket wanted to go home to Wabethe. He didn't really know if Wabethe was the woman who had died. But he knew that his silence would speak to Blue Jacket better than words. He had learned the power of silence from the great chief's example, and now it was a part of his own strength.

Blue Jacket handed Davey a black velveteen vest to put on over his grey-dun doeskin shirt. Davey had rubbed it over and over with ashes and charcoal and when he put it on, he felt more handsome than his ma had ever seen him.

When the chief was ready, Davey brought him his horse. "This is our chance, Davey." Blue Jacket stepped his left foot into Davey's cupped palms. As he was boosted up, he slowly lifted his leg over the horse's back. He didn't complain about the pain that must be jarring his bones, or the glare of sunlight in his weakened eyes. "We will work things out with Wayne and have our hunting lands back in peace."

Some soldiers stopped their digging to wave goodbye as Davey and Blue Jacket urged their horses forward with heads up, and great expectations back in the chief's eyes.

At Greenville, about a day's journey from Fort Wayne, an ample council house sat on a tract of ground cleared of trees and brush. Soldiers were passing out sparkling pieces of glass—blue, green, and red—to the Indians gathered there.

It was August 3, 1795. Blue Jacket sat tall and straight on a dappled grey pony, given to him by the Miamis' chief. Davey felt a surge of pride as he took his place by his noble father.

General Anthony Wayne's voice rose above the Indian crowd stretching far before him on the green lawn. "You will have the privilege of hunting and fishing in the Ohio River but you may not cross over it."

Davey faced the tribes and repeated Wayne's words in Shawnee with strong fire.

"You will have twenty-five thousand square miles of this land. There will be sixteen tracts within the present Indian territory." The rapturous words poured from the pompous little general, his face flushed over a tightly buttoned uniform collar. "These tracts will be six miles square and we will build forts on them."

Build forts on them! Davey moved closer to Blue Jacket. What did he mean *build forts on them?* thought Davey. How could the Indians hunt freely with American forts on their land.

"You will receive goods to equal one thousand, six hundred, sixty-six dollars for all the tribes, and an annual allowance." He continued. "Your individual allowance will equal eight hundred twenty-five dollars in goods." Wayne wore a benevolent smile.

Davey studied Blue Jacket's eyes. They were empty. His shoulders slumped.

The chiefs' talk sounded like rumbling, murmuring drums.

"Part of the territory they have granted us lies in the swamp," said Blue Jacket. He watched the happy Indians receive their glittering trinkets and shell beads. He lowered his head.

"Say something, Blue Jacket. Don't let them get away with this." Davey beat his fist against his hand. He could feel his heart ache as if it were one with the chief's.

"It was for this that Wayne asked me to gather all the Shawnees here." Blue Jacket closed his eyes against Davey's inquiring expression. "We will wait until our winter hunting is completed. When the rivers once again swell with the melting snow then we will leave our lands."

Davey stood motionless and watched the chiefs nod agreement, mount their horses and sadly turn toward home.

11

✛

Home

News of Sun-Will-Shine's death greeted them as they rode into the Shawnee camp across from Fort Defiance. She must have suspected what was going to happen, thought Davey.

Black Wolf lurked behind his mother's wegiwa. He darted from Davey's view.

"We heard," said Davey, walking toward him.

Black Wolf shrugged. "Why do you come to me?" He pushed Davey out of the way, then turned and planted his feet in front of him. "Nothing has gone right for me since you came to our village."

"It was you who brought me here, remember?"

Black Wolf threw a wild punch.

Davey ducked.

"White men are evil. You took my brother from me." Black Wolf swung again. His arm made a huge arc and connected with the side of Davey's head.

Davey staggered and fell to one knee. Then he lunged from a crouch for Black Wolf, grasping for his midsection.

Black Wolf managed to turn and avoid Davey's grasp. They circled each other, weaving from foot to foot.

Davey knew they were in a fight now.

Black Wolf seemed to know too, and danced around waiting for an opportunity to strike again. Awkwardly pushing, ducking, weaving, just missing contact, he seemed to be losing his nerve waiting for Davey's blow. "Come on, white boy," he taunted nervously.

Rage was growing in Davey, anticipating Black Wolf's next move. His heart thumped. He could feel it pumping wildly. He was losing his control. Panting, they faced each other. Davey swung, struck Black Wolf solidly in the head, and knocked him down.

Black Wolf grunted as he hit the ground. Then struggled to his feet and wrapped his arms around Davey's chest.

Davey felt the Mohawk's greasy muscles against his ribs. Davey's lean frame was tough as steel. He slid from Black Wolf's grasp, and switched the hold from behind.

With a sudden twist Black Wolf freed his hand and came down on Davey's neck like a cutting edge. Davey fell but tripped Black Wolf as he started to run. Anger seethed in him for all the encounters he'd had with this evil scout. *He's not getting away with this,* Davey thought. He leaped through the air, landed on Black Wolf and grabbed for the knife in his belt. The blade glistened as he held the cold steel to Black Wolf's neck. "I lost my mother too, you dirty Mohawk. She died because of the likes of you."

Tears welled in Black Wolf's eyes. "You still have your brother—I have not one." He gasped for air.

Suddenly Davey realized what he was doing. He leaped up and hurled the knife far out into the river.

Black Wolf sat up, wheezing.

"White Wolf could never have been your brother!" Davey turned his back to the scout.

"He was my half brother. My mother Sun-Will-Shine was married to Mohawk chief who died in battle. He was my father. Then she was wife of Shawnee, and White Wolf was their son. I did not like him. Now I wish him to be here with me."

Davey faced him.

Black Wolf's cheeks seemed to swell, tears running unchecked now.

"I want my brother here, too." Davey collected himself, pushing strands of sweaty hair from his eyes. "Were you with your mother when she died?"

"No. She slept. She was tired lately. I noticed that." Black Wolf's voice wandered off.

Davey thought Black Wolf hadn't noticed his mother much, not like he had noticed his ma. He always knew when she was tired or sick. But is must be hard for Black Wolf now, thinking about all he should have done. Just as it was hard for Davey to wonder if he could have saved his own ma's life.

They walked to the council house where the funeral for the peace woman was being prepared. Late summer clouds made shadows on the hills. Mottled shades of green lay in checkerboard patterns across the flatlands. The dismal chanting had begun. Davey left the council house and scanned the horizon.

Black Wolf's loss drew Davey into the past — the memories of a life he'd thought he could put behind him. New thoughts started taking shape. Maybe he couldn't have done anything back then to stop those renegades. Maybe Blue Jacket was right after all. *You can't change the past.*

It was late afternoon when he decided to go back. Purple wildflowers traced the old trail along the Tiffin. He hurried past the clump of woods, the gnarled sumac, the trail overgrown with clutching vines. He strained to see the blurred outline of a fieldstone chimney all strangled with weeds.

There it stood on the gentle stream, crumbling fieldstone covered with dense crabapple. A sharp pain stabbed his heart.

Deliberately, he made himself turn toward the place by the river. He fell flat down on the prickly ground hardly able to make out the graves covered with weeds. "Ma, Pa," he sobbed, I wanted to warn you. I'm sorry." He jumped down the bank and splashed through the water over sun-dappled stones, retrieved two smooth rocks bigger then his palms, and smashed them into the clay soil, till they stood, marking the place. "Ma, I lost Michael. Maybe Uncle Henry's got him. I guess you know where he is anyway. Maybe he's with you. I'm gonna stay here for awhile, Ma, and fix the place up again. I think I'm Indian, Ma. I feel good being Indian. They've been kind to me."

He laughed at the thought of throwing his knife away in the river; the way he must have looked dancing around like he didn't know whether to punch Black Wolf or not. It reminded him of the time Ma told them to go out in the back yard and fight out their argument. When they got out there neither one of them could hit the other. They'd swing and push a little, but ended up just settling things and going off in the woods together to look for trails.

He shook off the memories and got back to planning. He would split planks for the doors, make window blinds and tables like Pa showed him. The door hinges and latch would be wood. "I'll attach a string like you did so friends can raise the latch from outside and come in."

Crunching through the last leaves of fall, he circled the cabin site imagining warm cozy fires, the butter churn thumping, Pa laughing. He smelled his ma's baked bread and wild game cooking. The poplar still shimmered silver by the place where his bedroom window had been. The tree seemed smaller now.

There would be a loft with a sloped ceiling reached by a wooden ladder, a kitchen, bedroom and parlor — the 'best room' as Ma had called it. A candle and grease lamp would be in the best room window.

Davey heard a thump, then a swishing noise. Black Wolf came through the thicket holding out a charred school book. "Book burned," he said.

Davey held the book against his chest. "I can us this, Black Wolf."

"They don't want me at the village anymore. I haven't been with them since I tried to burn the fort." Black Wolf hunched close to Davey. "Can I stay with you?"

Davey looked at Black Wolf's swollen face, smelled his sweat. He wondered if he could trust him now.

"I will help you, Seapessee."

Davey's eyes were measuring him. "You'll work hard if you stay here."

"I am happy," said the swarthy Indian, a smile replacing an ugly frown.

As October frost touched the leaves, Black Wolf appeared from the woods each day to help Davey build his cabin. They chopped trees sixteen inches thick for the foundation, just the way Pa had done it.

Davey and Black Wolf grasped a log the length of the

house and laid it parallel to another log. They notched the logs for walls, then fit them tightly together. The notches locked the logs in place. They clinked and daubed the open spaces between the logs with mud to shut out the cold. Pa would have been proud. Working at the site of his sorrow, Davey began to feel better about himself.

They made beds of tree boughs and covered them with wolf skins. They finished the loft and stored blackberries, walnuts and roots in the eaves. It was almost winter when the cabin finally stood, clean and straight on the cleared square of land by the shallow Tiffin River.

As nippy winds blew, Davey made an oil lamp out of hickory bark, bear oil and a piece of cloth. He stuck the cloth in the container and lit it with a flint. He was admiring the soft yellow glow of the first light in the cabin when he saw the latch move.

The door opened. "My father!" Davey stretched his arm toward Blue Jacket. Black Wolf told me you had gone to visit the Ottawas in the south."

Blue Jacket walked over to the mellowed walnut wood bow hung by the door.

"It is Black Wolf's," said Davey.

"You are friends now? Should you not be careful of his wiley tricks?"

"He seems different since Sun-Will-Shine died." Davey brought a chair to the thin, weary chief. "Here, sit down."

"You have decided to live here and not at the village by the Maumee?"

Davey nodded. "I don't know exactly why, Blue Jacket. After the treaty I just needed time to think about who I am."

"Don't stay away too long, my son." Blue Jacket leaned into Davey seated next to him in the best room. His voice was thin. "There has been talk of Washington sending settlers to our country here by Lake Erie. They will have to drain this swampland, build roads, if they plan to live here."

"This is true."

"Our people have made camp at the forks until the rivers swell. They need us more than ever."

"Yes," said Davey, "I will come back some day."

"I have heard that our brave scout, Tecumseh, plans to try again to get the land back. Did you know he did not come to the treaty?"

"Yes, I knew." Davey studied the still tall, handsome chief with square jaw and crystal blue eyes. How he had tried to be just like him, but where was that strong man now? What would he do, he wondered.

"It may be moons before I see you again," said Blue Jacket, "Let's ride." He led the way outside.

Davey whistled for his pony. She trotted smartly to his side, her silver mane bouncing.

"Polly came back to the forks." Blue Jacket mounted the stallion and eased his horse down the bank.

Davey jerked to a halt. He wasn't sure he had heard what Blue Jacket had said. "Where is Michael? Did she find him? Did they go east on the boats?"

"I think she got herself mixed up with this white fur trader," Blue Jacket continued. "He's with her. She won't talk about Michael."

"Please forgive me, Chief Blue Jacket but I must know if Michael is safe. Do I have your permission to leave you now?" The chief nodded and Davey grabbed his pony's mane and plunged through the creek. She splashed sheets of water as they crossed Tiffin, threading through brush by the river, never shortening her stride.

As he approached the wide waters of the Maumee, he could see the cluster of wegiwas nestled against the bank. Cows huddled in the cold sunlight. A group of boys chased some girls carrying their ghostleg dolls. He dismounted and led his pony among the wegiwas.

Wabethe came running toward him, waving her hand in the air. "Davey, Davey, where have you been? We've missed you."

"And I have missed you too, Wabethe. I have rebuilt my cabin. But I will someday return to live among you again. Have you seen Polly Meadows?"

"She left. Davey, when she saw the traders' camp all burned down and the huge fort at the forks, she threw up her hands as if she didn't understand what was happening to her."

"Did she tell you about Michael? What did she say, Wabethe?"

"She refused to speak of Michael. She and the man just wanted to leave. Oh, Davey, I'm so sorry!"

"Why didn't she stay to see me?"

"Davey Seapessee, Polly cared only for herself. She wouldn't answer Blue Jacket's questions. She is hiding something."

"Did she know I was here?"

"Yes. Maybe that is why she left so quickly." Wabethe swept her skirt to the side and sat on the huge stump on the apple tree that once stood so grandly by Sun-Will-Shine's bark cabin. "Blue Jacket will go south again soon to mourn his own white brother." She straightened her back and tucked her legs under her. "Don't think about Polly, Davey. She probably found Michael and took him east as Ironside and you had planned."

Davey answered in short breaths. His face felt drawn. He pushed his hair out of his eyes, raking the stray locks straight back from his forehead. "I have to know for sure. I need Michael now." His pony stamped her hoof restlessly on the hard ground.

"I know," Wabethe said thoughtfully, lingering her gaze on him as if she could read his very soul. "But if he is with your uncle, maybe he wouldn't understand your life here. Maybe it would be best to leave him alone. Even if you knew where he was."

Davey noticed the lines around Wabethe's mouth. She looked older, too. Passing shell beads between her calloused fingers, a faraway look came to rest in her dove-like eyes. She rearranged her legs, crossing them under her, then seemed to disappear out of her body.

Davey had more questions. But he rose without her notice and mounted his pony, resting his hands on his hips, guiding her slowly along the river with his knees.

Blue Jacket was gone when he got home. Black Wolf had already been there and taken his bow down from the hook. Davey was alone. He had never missed Michael so much.

The last part of the day was still sparkling and beautiful, full of buttery sunlight and slick gold and red leaves. Davey's eyes clouded with hostile thoughts of Polly, and of her friend the fur trader. He had trusted her. Did she even find Michael? Not knowing was the worst part.

Moonlight traded places with the sun. Davey hit the wall with his fist. He threw open the door, strode to the bank, grabbed a rock and hurled it into the stream. Circles spread wider and wider until they disappeared. It seemed the world was like that, widening in circles ever bigger till you couldn't see where they began or ended. He knew one thing; he would stay with the people who loved him.

Black Wolf came back. He fried a slab of bacon for supper. "What is it, Seapessee?" The misery must have been plain on Davey's face.

"I think Michael is dead."

12

+

Michael

Storm clouds gathered and rain chattered on the roof. Black Wolf poured herbs into boiling water, sending off a sweet pungent smell.

They sat in the gold light till Davey spoke again. "I was going to teach him to trap and chase buffalo."

"Teach him to be Indian," Black Wolf moaned.

"No. Well, yes. I don't know. Just keep him with me, make him glad to stay here and do things I like."

"Maybe it's just as well." Black Wolf took the boiling pot from the hook above the fire, lifted a horn spoon and poured broth.

"What do you mean?" Davey knew what Black Wolf meant. He'd never get Michael to stay if he didn't want to.

"The bird doesn't fly unless you open your hand. If you keep him there against his will he will die," Black Wolf said.

Davey felt miserable. "I'll never see him again anyway. I know that now. My heart tells me."

It was dawn when he heard the noise. He got up from

his bed and slide down the ladder from the loft. The wind swirled fallen leaves by the door as it burst open. Blue Jacket stood there. Davey glanced to the chief's side. A boy stood very close to him, his sandy hair brushing Blue Jacket's arm.

Another figure, tall and heavy, was in the shadows. The big man wore a blue suit and white bosom ruffles. He had Ma's kind eyes, but his mouth turned down at the corners. Moving past Davey into the best room, his silky gray hair rippled across his shoulders.

Blue Jacket put his arm around Davey. "They came to our village. They looked for your burned-out cabin." He reached for the young boy's hand.

Davey's eyes glistened with unspent tears not believing what he saw.

Michael looked searchingly at him.

A rush of hot tears blinded Davey for an instant.

"It's all right, son," said the big man, thrusting his palm at Davey. "I'm your Uncle Henry."

Davey shook it. His uncle's voice had the same lyrical quality of his ma's.

Black Wolf tried to disappear out the door, but Davey grabbed his arm and pulled him over to Michael. "This is Black Wolf."

"I'll put the pot back on the fire, Seapessee," said Black Wolf.

Davey studied Michael. His hair was straight and cut short—gone were the sandy curls. He had grown taller.

"I can't believe you're here." Michael's voice was older, and had a cultured tone. "We thought you were killed." His eyes widened with disbelief as he stared at Davey' long black hair, the sharp claw dangling from his neck, strong shoulders bronzed by the sun.

Davey touched his hand. He had the same clean smell as he used to, like hot sun on his hair.

Michael tried to embrace him, but Davey held him at arm's length, looking at him, feeling his shoulders through the pressed white shirt he wore. Holding him away like that, he felt some resentment that Michael should walk in after all his worrying — when he'd finally got use to the idea that he'd never see him again. He wasn't ready to hug him yet.

"Davey, George Washington sent Uncle Henry here to build a road through the swamp, and we found you," said Michael.

Uncle Henry spoke. "When they brought Michael to us in the east, my tannery business was ruined by the war. Money was gone, so the government offered us a land grant to settle in Cincinnati.

"We began our journey in wagons over the Pennsylvania roads, took a flatboat down the Ohio, passing shores with honey trees and spicewoods all along..."

"You forgot about Fort Pitt, Uncle Henry."

"That's right. We went from Jersey, past Easton, through the Alleghenies to Pittsburg."

Davey listened to the story about the boat that had to be built before they could start their journey down the Monongahela, Susquehana and Ohio Rivers.

"I was almost grabbed to be a soldier at Fort Pitt, Davey. Maybe we can live there in the big city someday." Michael's cheeks flushed with excitement the way they used to.

Davey winced. "Where did Polly find you?"

"At the Miamis' camp down the Tiffin. Those bad Indians carried me there in the sack. They sold me to the Miamis." Michael's eyes clouded. "That's when Polly and Mr. Moore found me."

"Guess you're afraid of Indians now."

"I was scared when I was in that sack! But Mr. Moore convinced the chief he was a friend of George Ironside, and he let me go." Michael continued his story about Moore putting them on the big English ship in the Detroit harbor, and going back down to Ironside's camp. "Polly explained to me about looking for Uncle Henry back east. She told me you sent her. I was scared when we got on the ship, but then it was fun sailing to Buffalo across the Great Lakes."

"How did you find Henry?"

Michael continued his account of Polly leaving him with a man at the government building. He was a friend of Henry's. He said he put him on another boat headed for Jersey where Uncle Henry met him and took him home. "I didn't remember Uncle Henry, but then he told me all about Ma when they were growing up as kids."

"Now I'll take care of you, too, Davey. You won't have to stay with the Indians anymore." Uncle Henry reached for him.

Davey stared at Henry. "The Shawnees are my family," he said.

"It's your right to do as you please," Henry said.

They sat talking most of the day, until the gold fire-light filled the best room and spilled into the darkness of the kitchen.

Michael leaned against Davey, talking non-stop about the fort at Pitt. "There were twenty-four nine-pounder cannons and rows of six pounders protecting her rear." Finally his voice trailed to a whisper.

Davey noticed the fine clothes Michael was wearing.

He could tell it was too late for his younger brother to want to stay with Indians. He wouldn't even ask him.

Gathering Michael awkwardly in his arms, Davey laid him on the furs stretched by the fire. "*Nepaalo,* lie down," he said.

Uncle Henry climbed the ladder to the loft. Blue Jacket and Black Wolf slipped out into the night.

Davey lay next to Michael, the way he used to.

"Have you ever killed anyone?" Michael was just barely awake.

Davey stared at the ceiling. Something inside made him want to say yes, that he had been brave enough to kill for his Indian brother as he would be for Michael. His hands went clammy. Keeping something from Michael was like not telling himself the truth. "No," he said simply. Suddenly he felt relief—Michael would never have understood his killing.

In the silence, Davey thought Michael was asleep.

"Do Indians believe in heaven?"

It grew cold in the shadows. Davey pulled up a red blanket and tucked it around Michael's shoulders. "They don't call it that, but they do."

"Do you believe Ma and Pa are there?"

Davey lay down on his side facing Michael. "If there is one, Ma and Pa are there."

"You're just like Uncle Henry. He doesn't know either."

"Nobody comes back, Michael. How could we know for sure?" He waited.

"Jesus came back."

"I really don't believe Ma and Pa could have taught us all those things and have it not be true. They believed it, Michael."

"I miss them, Davey."

Davey couldn't look at him. He wondered how Michael would feel if he knew all the things Davey knew.

"Will you always be here?"

Davey wasn't sure if he meant here on earth or just here in the cabin by the Tiffin. But he didn't have to answer. He wrapped his arms around Michael, his chin resting on his brother's head. He didn't move until he could hear Michael's deep regular breathing. *I'll keep him here with me forever.* His heart ached to keep him there. *I'll keep him just long enough to teach him all I know.* The truth kept tossing him back and forth. *I can't let him go again.* But then Davey imagined Michael's dancing eyes turning dull and brooding if he had to stay here among the Indians. *Oui-shi-cat-to-oui,* be strong, he told himself.

Davey wiped the tears from his cheek, but they kept rolling down on Michael's sandy head. No one was looking, and it felt so good to cry.

He slipped his arm from under Michael's head and watched him sleep. Thoughts streamed through his mind. When the renegades set his cabin on fire, he wanted to be brave and save his parents. He wanted to catch the renegades and snatch the sack out of their hands, but he would have been killed in the attempt.

Now he understood that it wasn't his fault. He couldn't have stopped them; he couldn't have saved his ma and pa. All these months he had been trying to prove his bravery, when being brave was just doing what you have to do. And he had.

Davey's tense muscles relaxed. Peace came over him and the dark feeling of guilt disappeared, like the morning mist that burns off the sun.

Warm, orange firelight melted into a misty glow from Davey's oil lamp. The sooty smell of wood burning reminded him of his days at Blue Jacket's side in the giant wegiwa. Now, in this cabin he had build from the ashes, he found himself. He knew who he was.

Davey didn't know what was going to happen next, but he and Michael were together and that was all that mattered. Gently he lay his head next to Michael's and whispered, "*Ni-kao-nao-nah*, my brother."